THE GROOMSMAN
Marina Hanna

This book is a work of fiction. All content is a product of the author's overactive imagination.
Any resemblance to actual persons, living or deceased, are entirely coincidental.

Copyright © 2021 Marina Hanna
All rights reserved.

CHAPTER 1

Lauren

I'm not sure what wakes me, but as soon as I'm roused from the most satisfying, peaceful slumber I've had in months, I remember exactly where I am and how I got here. I look up at the ceiling to admire the rainbow of light created by the stray ray of sunshine hitting the ornate crystal light fitting as it filters through a gap in the curtains.

As I glance to my right, my eyes fall on the hunk of a man lying next to me, blissfully sleeping like a baby. Jesus, he even snores perfectly. It's slow and infrequent, almost like a sigh.

He makes me want to lie beside him and spoon. Fall asleep in his arms and be engulfed in the protection and comfort they offer and stay there for all eternity.

But never kid a kidder, right. I know what this is. A night filled with lust and desire with an acquaintance. An encounter with no expectations. A silent agreement that there will be no exchange of phone numbers. No promises to call. Just two people connecting to satisfy their sexual needs.

Of course there are some rules that should be adhered

to at weddings, such as dress code. Not wearing white. Not upstaging the bride. But wedding hook-ups are expected. I don't think there are any rules against that. It's just two people who are insanely attracted to each other, giving in to their desires. The bridesmaid and the groomsman keeping with tradition and doing the dirty.

I study his facial features. Although his eyes are closed, I recall how penetrating they are. I recall how an eager look flashed in his cinnamon-brown eyes every time they caught mine. They blazed with such desire as they raked boldly over my body. They gleamed with satisfaction with each touch as he explored each and every contour of my body.

His generous lips—and trust me, they're very generous—are curved at the corners with the beginnings of a smile. Perhaps he's dreaming about last night. What images are running through his mind? What sensations is he remembering?

My memory serves me very well, and I know with certainty that any images playing in his mind are not pure. They're lecherous. There was a hunger that made us desperate to feed our salacious appetites for each other. I feel my skin tingle at the mere memory of our night together.

But when I recall his kisses, while his mouth covered my mine, there was a surprising gentleness. His lips were warm and soft as they nibbled at my earlobe. They were exploratory as he took his time to kiss each erogenous zone of my body.

I smile to myself as I recall how his square jaw clenched when he was pounding into me, and the grin that splayed across his face at his satisfaction when we simultaneously hurtled to the finish line, both crying out in pleasant exhaustion.

I sit up in order to fully appreciate him, because let's face it, who knows how long it will be before I have amazing sex like this again. Who knows how long it will be before I find a man so insanely sexy, so ravishingly handsome, so magnificently skilled in satisfying me? I'd go as far as saying I'd sell my soul to have more nights with *the groomsman*.

One bare muscular arm lies across his body while the other is tucked under his pillow. I admire the intricate rose tattoo on the back of his hand, which starts on his wrist but doesn't quite reach his knuckles; I wonder if it has a special significance. And since I've spent the entire last six hours or so exploring his beautifully hard, toned body, I know that it's his only tattoo.

His dark brown hair is ruffled and damp, but I resist the temptation to reach out and lightly swipe the tendrils away from his forehead. Too personal, too familiar. Ironic really.

The sheet covers the lower part of his torso, and I take a moment longer to appreciate his upper body, his chiselled abs and smooth chest, which still glistens with sweat from the physical exertion of our antics. Would he wake if I ran my tongue along his six-pack?

Before I do anything outrageously inappropriate, although judging from last night's escapades, I suspect it's a little late to be acting all prim and proper, I reluctantly slink out of the comfy, inviting, king-size bed.

Trying to make as little noise as possible, I grab my bridesmaid dress from the heap on the floor and get dressed while I internally berate myself. Because I can't believe at twenty-eight years of age I'm going to have to do the walk of shame along the corridor of a five-star hotel in central London, where yesterday my best friend, Jules, had a second wedding reception after getting married a few weeks earlier in The Hamptons. She married the love of her life, her boss, Adam Foster. She finally got her happy ever after.

Me, not so much. After finding out six months down the line that my last relationship was a fraud because, unbeknown to me, he was married, I've kept myself well and truly single.

Of course I've had casual hook-ups; the last being the hunky Jason Momoa lookalike barman from our regular drinking haunt. And even though we both knew at the time that it wasn't going to be anything serious, he's restored my faith in men just a little, because it wasn't just a case of *wham-bam-thank-you-ma'am*. He was upfront from the beginning. He didn't do long term because he never envisaged staying in one place long enough to put down roots.

But for the few weeks we were sleeping together, he treated me like a princess. He still looks out for me at the bar when guys hover, giving his approval with a nod or his disapproval with a raised eyebrow and subtle shake of the head. I consider him a dear friend, and I'll be sad when he does finally move on. Funny how things turn out.

But I seem to have surpassed myself this time, and I can't even blame the drink because I somehow managed to stay sober. I only had three glasses of champagne and ensured that I spread out my intake during the entire night.

And since I wasn't drunk, I can remember every single ravishing detail of last night. Every touch, every look. Every kiss his moist lips peppered me with. Every feral sound that escaped our lungs.

I let out a silent sigh at the fact that last night will be consigned to mere memories—albeit exquisite memories—forever lingering on the edges of my mind. It's safe to say that with one night, he's managed to ruin me for all other men.

Once I've put my dress on, I grab my shoes, stuff my underwear into my clutch bag ready to tiptoe out, just as my phone starts to vibrate.

"Shit," I say soft and low as I fumble in my bag. I drop the phone when I'm startled by his words, his voice deep and husky, causing his words of last night to ring in my ears— *I want to taste you—I can't wait to be inside you—I'm going to fuck you like you've never been fucked before.*

"Where do you think you're going?"

I curse under my breath, plaster a smile on my face and turn to look at the hunk of a *groomsman* in the bed.

"I'm heading back to my room to shower and get a change of clothes before I go down to breakfast."

He sits up, allowing the sheet to fall low enough to expose his deep V-shaped cut, but my eyes are unable to avoid moving lower to the glaringly obvious tenting of the sheet and the fact that he's standing to attention. Making no attempt to hide it, there's amusement in his eyes as he looks at me, a smirk on his face as he places his hands strategically on his hips.

"Isn't that a dereliction of your bridesmaid duties? I haven't finished with you yet. What about what I want for breakfast?"

I shrug. "Call room service."

"What I'm craving isn't on the menu."

"And what exactly is it you're craving for breakfast?"

He throws the sheet back completely, and my eyes immediately fixate on his hardness. I can't help licking my lips at the sight, as I'm unable to stop every detail of last night flooding my mind. I know exactly what he can do with that thing. I know how long he can keep it up. I know what it feels like inside me. I remember precisely how my body welcomed him. How I ached in anticipation. How he made me gasp at my own arousal.

He swings his legs out of bed and stands, bold as brass, not the least bit embarrassed to be standing there naked, but then why would he be. His body is perfection. Everything about him denotes strength and power, a sense of self. He knows exactly how unbelievably capable he is.

He steps around the bed and comes towards me, and without using his hands, he presses his naked body against mine. I can feel his hard length through the thin satin fabric of my dress, pressing against my thigh, making me inhale sharply at the feeling of my skin tingling pleasurably.

"I recall something about promising to eat you out for breakfast, and I never break my promises."

He keeps eye contact with me, never faltering. His eyes are on fire, filled with want, and it seems to increase our connection and the level of intensity, making me unable to wrench myself away, enjoying the intimacy of this moment.

Clearly used to multitasking, he places kisses on my neck as his fingers push the straps of my floor-length dress off my shoulders, allowing it to glide down my body and fall to the floor, pooling at my feet. My hands instinctively hold on to his broad shoulders as I step out of my dress.

He goes from top to bottom, licking the crevice between my breasts, sucking the peaks of my hardened buds.

Then he lowers himself to kneel before me, grabs by buttocks, digging his fingers into my flesh and proceeds to do exactly what he promised; eat me out—taking his time to kiss my inner thighs. Using his mouth to suck and his tongue to lick, making slow movements that become faster and firmer as I moan with pleasure.

My fingers are digging into the flesh of his shoulders, grasping on for dear life as my body responds to the seduction of his passion. "Oh God."

As I'm about to reach my climax, he suddenly stops. Picks me up, takes the few steps back to the bed, and places me gently down in the centre.

He grabs a condom from the nightstand, and in no time he's lowering his body over mine, placing himself at my entrance, sliding into me as I gasp from the sheer ecstasy as his hardness fills me, throbbing, gyrating, thrusting inside of me. I arch my back to meet each and every thrust.

"You feel fucking amazing."

I can't help but vocalise my pleasure. "Never… felt… so… good."

"Oh yeah. That's it, baby, let me hear your sexy little moans."

As I hurtle towards my orgasm, he thrusts one final time, letting out a groan of pleasure at his release, then collapses breathless beside me.

His eyes are closed, his hands resting on his stomach, as he sighs in pleasant exhaustion, and his breaths finally become even.

A warmth spreads across me as I imagine us together like this again. What I wouldn't give to have a man like this all of my own. I'm unable to stop myself from letting my imagination run wild as I picture us together as a couple. I've paid my dues. Is it too much to ask the gods who've dangled this man in front of me, enticing me with his virility, captivating me with his mere presence, to let me keep him for more than one night?

I lean down and kiss him softly on the forehead, then get out of bed and quietly get dressed to leave and go to my room down the hall.

Whilst getting dressed, I remember I'm going to have to do the walk of shame. Hardly ideal but I'm a big girl, I'll live. I also can't ignore how cliché this whole situation is.

"The bridesmaid hooking up with the groomsman, so bloody original," I mutter to myself.

"I know what you're thinking, and there's nothing cliché about what we did last night, and into the early hours of this morning. If that's cliché, then I'm all for it," he says.

I shake my head dubiously as I look at him. "Really? Do you even recall my name?" Call me cynical, but I'm not going to ignore the obvious.

He sits up and leans against the headboard, his arms at his sides, hands palm down on the mattress. "What the fuck do you take me for? I may be easy, but I'm not an arsehole, *Lauren*." A smile tips the corners of his mouth as he says my name, like it's some kind of achievement to have remembered. "And the fact that you were repeatedly screaming my name as you came does wonders for a guy's ego."

I can't help smiling at him, secretly pleased that even though I'm probably just another notch on his bed post, at least I'll be memorable. He, on the other hand, will definitely be unforgettable. In fact, I'll go so far as to say that I suspect I'll have a smile on my face for months to come.

"I had a great night. Thanks for… everything." I hasten my exit before I say anything to ruin this, such as *please can we see each other again,* but I pause at the door just a fraction, hoping against hope that he'll stop me and ask for my phone number—ask to see me again. But he doesn't. And even though I knew the score going into this, it's with a tinge of disappointment that I let the door silently close behind me.

Mark

I'm lying next to the sexiest woman I've ever met, and after having the best night of my life, I'm not prepared to let her walk out without having one more taste, one more helping. And what a sweet taste she is.

As tempting as it is to ask her not to leave, after finally letting her go, and as the door closes behind her, I'm left alone with my thoughts. I can't ever recall a time when I questioned my feelings after a good fuck. But for some inexplicable reason, the only thoughts running through my mind are whether this is more than just physical attraction.

I've had plenty of one-night stands in my time. As sad as it may sound, at thirty-seven years old, I've come to relish the easy hook-up, the no-strings-attached sex; it's a means to an end. Of course if I've had a great time with a particular woman, I'll gladly see her again for a repeat performance. But I don't have room in my life for a relationship right now. And Lauren Roberts is a woman who deserves to be cherished and adored. The best thing I can do for both of us is put some space between us. Despite her being one of Jules's best friends, we haven't had much interaction up to now, so I'm sure keeping my distance will not be a problem. That's why I didn't ask for her number. I'm confident that after a few days, we'll both recognise that things were just in the moment.

The problem is that she's unlocked something within me. My flesh prickled at her touch. My heartbeat pulsed rhythmically from the excitement of touching her.

She's been gone only a few minutes, and already I know I'm going to need to taste more. My taste buds are aroused. I'm going to need to satisfy the craving my tongue has to lavishly lick her juices; I'm going to need to satisfy the want my hardness has to be inside her again.

I want to hear her laughter ringing in my ears. I want to be the one to make her laugh. I want to be around her playfulness and her passion. But I know I have no right to want those things. Because I only have room in my life for one woman.

As the vivid recollections of the last few hours burn in my mind, my phone vibrates. I push myself up and sit on the edge of the bed, then reach for the phone on the nightstand. I feel an instant smile overtake my face and my heart bursting with love when I look at the caller ID.

"Hey, Angel."

CHAPTER 2
Lauren

Even though the corridor has the thickest, plushest carpet you can imagine, I still find myself tiptoeing barefoot along the corridor to my room like a cat burglar. It's a real treat beneath my feet as my toes sink into the softness of the carpet.

Since we're all on the same floor, I consider myself pretty lucky not to have run into any of the other members of the wedding party. I suspect Adam and Jules are still cocooned in their room between the sheets. Rachel, I would hazard a guess, is already up and raring to go as she's going straight to the airport from the hotel to meet her fiancé, Tom.

Once in my room, I head straight to the bathroom. As I take a look in the mirror, I can see the remnants of my make-up. I bite my bottom lip to stop the tingle as I have a flash back to Mark and I doing all kinds of acrobatic positions. God, if that wasn't the best night I've had in a long time. The sex was amazing.

I knew what I was getting myself into. Jules had warned me about Mark Taylor. She explained to me his reputation of never dating seriously. But I couldn't help myself. From the moment I saw him in his tux, standing tall and powerful, strong and sexy, it seemed to make him even more attractive. I knew the moment I saw him I wanted something to happen. I knew I wanted him.

We started with subtle flirtatious glances. When we were seated next to each other for dinner, we continued with teasing conversation. This was followed by light touches of the arm, a brush of the hands, and him scooting his chair closer to mine, leaning in so that our bodies were close, enabling him to whisper in my ear; *you look incredible. I'm picturing us naked together right now.*

It's when it progressed to under the table touching, the feel of his warm hand lightly resting on my thigh, as if that's where it was meant to be, where it wanted to be, where it belonged. That was a very satisfying feeling, and that's when I knew I wouldn't be able to deny myself.

I've had a dry spell lately. I want it—badly. So is it any wonder that I hooked up with the groomsman when he exudes such confidence that you just know you're in for the time of your life? That's when I knew, without a shadow of doubt, that I would end up in his room.

The mere memory of last night has my cheeks flushed. I can still feel the warmth of his body covering mine, and as I glance at my reflection in the mirror, I smile to myself when I see the radiance showing in my face, then chuckle at the thought of what put it there. No doubt I'll be clinging to the memory like a life preserver. Something to keep me warm on a lonely night.

I slip out of my dress, tie my hair up, and have a quick shower. I change into skinny jeans, a T-shirt, comfy wedges, and pack up my things before heading down to breakfast.

I cross the lobby to leave my holdall in the luggage

room behind reception and head straight for the breakfast room where I join an enthusiastic Rachel, who seems to be chomping at the bit with impatience. I've barely sat down before she's waggling her brows at me. She can't stop her curiosity from getting the better of her.

"So, tell me about last night?"

I'm buttering my bagel. "What do you want to know exactly?"

"Was he as good as he looks he'd be?"

I place my knife down. "Rach, what kind of question is that? How does he look?" I take a bite of my bagel, chewing slowly as I await her reply. Curious to know what she thinks of him.

"Like he's a gentleman who will lavish all of his attention on you, but an animal who'll then ravish you to within an inch of your pleasure."

I almost choke on my food as I swallow. "You know what, it's a good thing Tom is back today because I think you're having withdrawal symptoms. To answer your question, yes, he does everything you would want and more, even things you didn't know you wanted."

She lowers her thick, dark lashes as her voice becomes filled with awe. She speaks into her coffee cup just before she's about to take a sip.

"Wow. That good. So, are you going to see him again?" Her eyes study my face over the rim of her cup.

"I doubt it, not in the sense you probably mean. He's one of Adam's closest friends so I'm sure I'll bump into him every now and then, but he didn't mention hooking up again, and he didn't ask for my phone number, so that'll be a big fat no."

She taps into the shell of her boiled egg with a teaspoon. "Is that disappointment I detect in the tone of your voice?"

I sigh and give a resigned shrug. "Yes. No. Oh I don't know. I guess it's just me facing the harsh reality of it. I mean, one-night stands very rarely materialise into anything serious, so I'm not holding my breath. It's just that the sex was so great. And he has a maturity to him but a playful side too. We didn't do very much talking, but when we did, conversation flowed easily. It was so refreshing not to feel awkward, even during the silences. It all felt very comfortable if that makes sense. Maybe it's simply because he's a few years older."

"It makes perfect sense. That's exactly how I felt about Tom and look at us now."

"Rach, he's your high school sweetheart. You've been together since forever; you're engaged for crying out loud. He bloody well better be the one, otherwise I'll cut his bloody balls off."

"Hmm, you seem to have balls on the mind this morning."

There's a moment's silence before we both break into hysterical laughter causing a few heads to turn in our direction.

"All I'm saying is, it's a shame. I like him. But hey, C'est la vie, or more accurately, that's my life."

An hour later we leave the hotel, and I'm heading home in a cab for a lazy Sunday afternoon. Doing nothing but reminiscing about my night with Mark and the sheer ecstasy of being held in his strong arms with his hard body aligned with mine.

CHAPTER 3

Lauren

Deadlines and demanding clients keep me very busy over the next couple of weeks. There have been rumblings of dissatisfaction for a while from some of the creative team, me included, and when Jules jumped ship to work at Foster Advertising, the fuddy-duddy hierarchy at Miller Advertising finally sat up to take notice. They've pulled their heads out of their arses and taken on new clients, shaken things up a little. Much to the delight of myself and everyone else, we now have some juicy modern campaigns to work on.

My current campaign is for a company specialising in rubber. Silicone rubber to be precise. And to be even more specific, they manufacture every conceivable type of dildo. Vibrating, double-ended, strap-on, soft, hard. You name it, they do it.

Of course I'm throwing myself into this campaign wholeheartedly. I'm doing an extremely healthy amount of systematic investigation into studying the materials and the actual function of the products. But while this is all very pleasurable, it only serves to remind me of the last time I had the real thing in my hands, between my legs, and everywhere else for that matter.

It's been two weeks since my one-night stand with Mark, and I haven't been able to get him out of my mind. I've even resulted to stalking him online. Not in any unbalanced way, just a healthy curiosity.

I quickly established he has no Facebook or Instagram profile so, having recalled the name of his law firm, Taylor Mackintosh, I've checked out his profile on their website. I've taken a screenshot of his profile photo, and I look at his handsomeness last thing at night, which, along with the toys I'm testing for research, further fuels my fantasies.

***

I'm sitting in the conference room with Joshua Nolan, the extremely handsome CEO from the dildo company, to give him an update on my ideas, or rather my one idea. As soon as I came up with it, I swiftly discarded everything else, confident that this is the one. He's listening intently as I continue to outline my idea.

"I think we should keep the campaign simple. There's no need to explain what the product is or what it does. It's self-explanatory. Plus, bearing in mind we won't be doing TV ads, we need to think about what's acceptable for magazine placements. So I've come up with a short, catchy, to the point slogan, which we'll run alongside pictures of the product."

Joshua shifts in his chair. He quirks his brow questioningly. From the moment I took on this campaign, I prepared myself for the inevitable remarks that were bound to come from my colleagues. But I didn't expect it from the client.

One… two… three, and "Tell me, Lauren, have you tested our product yourself?"

I manage to keep myself composed and professional, not a flicker of surprise, not an ounce of annoyance is evident on my face. As I stare at him, he stares back, waiting.

I display the leisurely smile I've managed to cultivate for awkward or inappropriate situations and reply confidently. "Absolutely. And I can testify that the slogan is definitely not misleading, in any shape or form. There will be no complaints to the Advertising Standards Authority, I can assure you of that."

And noticing the wedding band on his finger, I know I shouldn't, but I can't help myself. "Perhaps your wife would like to avail herself and give you some feedback. I strongly recommend the Plough."

"I'm gay."

I'm undeterred. "Oh well then, I would recommend Wrecked, the double-ended dildo. I haven't actually tried it out myself, perhaps you could report back, let me know how it goes."

His outburst of laughter reverberates around the room until we're both in hysterics.

"I have to say, Lauren, working with you is extremely entertaining. And your slogan, positively fabulous. Works for both the hetero crowd and the gay community. I think it's brilliant."

"So I can proceed and get the campaign started?"

"Yes. I think we're onto a winner here."

We both stand and I walk him out before going back to my desk where I start playing around with some graphics for my slogan.

MEN: OPTIONAL.

Feeling the need to celebrate the client's pleasure, no pun intended, after work Rachel and I head to our usual watering hole. It's the restaurant bar where Jules encountered Adam for the first time. It's where I first clapped eyes on Mark, albeit briefly. It's where the Jason Momoa lookalike barman I had a fling with still works. Maybe I should revisit that; we ended things very amicably, no reason why we can't simply take up where we left off. But I quickly brush aside any contemplation of doing such a thing when I recall the downpour of fiery sensations Mark unleashed. Oh well, it would've been a rebound thing anyway. Because I really don't want to be with anyone but Mark again.

We're seated, handed our menus, and our drink orders are taken.

"So he hasn't called you at all? Are you sure you haven't missed the call? Why wouldn't he call you?"

I continue looking through the menu and answer without looking up. "I don't know Rach. Probably because he didn't ask for my number, remember, we've had this conversation. It was a one-night stand. You do know what the definition of that is don't you?"

"Of course I do. But I thought you looked good together dancing at the wedding reception. He only had eyes for you. I think you make a nice couple."

"Nice! Can't you use a better adjective than that? And besides, if what you're saying is actually correct, he only had eyes for me because I was probably one of the few single women there for him to hook up with."

"Why are you selling yourself short. You're a good catch. You're gorgeous and funny. You're independent—you have a career, your own apartment—guys like that. Why wouldn't he be interested?"

"Rach, I'm sorry to tell you this, but I think you need to realise not every man is as decent as Tom. Some men just want to get their leg over and wave you off when they're done. I'm not complaining, I had a great time too. It's just a shame that's all. I would've liked to see him again."

"See who?" says Jules as she finally waltzes in a little breathless and sits down at the table.

"About bloody time, I'm starving," I say.

"You could've started without me."

As if on cue our margaritas arrive, Jules orders sparkling water, and the three of us order a burger and fries.

"So, what were you talking about. More to the point, who were you talking about?"

"Nothing," I say

"Mark," Rachel blurts out as I scowl at her.

Jules's brows draw together in a confused expression, her voice rising an octave in surprise. "He hasn't called you?"

"Erm, no, but that's no great surprise since I didn't give him my phone number."

"But I gave it to him. He asked me for it a few days after the wedding reception."

Suddenly, Rachel's face lights up and her eyes widen with excitement. I glare at her, eyes narrowed and hardened. "Stop it," I say. "I know what you're thinking, but he hasn't called so take your cue from that."

"No," she says as her smile broadens, and she becomes more animated. "Look over there. Look who's just walked in." She gestures with her bobbing head towards the bar.

We follow her line of vision to see Mark and another guy taking a seat on the vacant stools at the bar.

"Oh, I should go over and say hello."

I don't have time to make any objections before Jules is up from the table and walking over to the bar, actually, in her condition it's more of a waddle, since she's six months pregnant.

Obviously, I can't resist stealing a glance, which despite not wanting to be caught, turns into a stare of curiosity.

He seems genuinely happy to see her. He stands and kisses her cheek. He introduces her to his friend, and she shakes his hand. Their conversation seems easy, engrossing.

She gestures with a wave of her hand to our table without looking, but Mark does look. His eyes are staring directly at me. It's a lingering look, and there's a brief moment when I think I detect laughter in his eyes as they wrinkle at the sides, as though he's playing a game. He doesn't take his eyes off me even as he reaches for his glass and takes a sip of his drink.

Jules says something, which makes him focus his attention back on her. They laugh, another kiss on the cheek, and she makes her way back to our table.

Rachel doesn't even wait for Jules to sit down before she puts the question to her. The question that I desperately want to know the answer to but am too cowardly to ask, because I want to continue with the charade of not really giving a shit.

"So what did he say?"

"Oh, this and that," she says matter-of-factly. "We more or less just talked about how I'm feeling and when the baby's due. Then I asked why he hasn't called you."

"Oh my God! I'm going to die of embarrassment. Please say you didn't." My humiliation is complete. Thank heavens for the low lighting that's hiding the blush in my cheeks.

Once again, Rachel comes through for me. "Well, why hasn't he? What's his excuse?"

"He didn't really give a reason. What he did say is that

it's an oversight he's determined to rectify very soon."

I sigh in despair at now feeling even more despondent. "Great, I'm an oversight. That's it. Change of subject." I put a stop to all Mark-related conversation there and then for the rest of our evening. I don't want to be reminded of what I'm missing out on—wishful thinking about what could have been.

But I'm only human after all, and curiosity gets the better of me when I find myself discreetly glancing over at Mark throughout the evening. Downhearted that he doesn't even cast a fleeting look in my direction. Disappointed when he finally leaves the bar.

My night with Rachel and Jules ends on a promise to meet up again soon, something that no doubt is going to become a little more difficult once Jules has her baby.

CHAPTER 4
Lauren

As soon as I get home I go through my nightly ritual. I take my make-up off. Brush my teeth and slip into my black cami and shorts set.

I walk to the bedroom window to close the navy curtains, which are accented with the moon and stars. As I do so, I notice there's a black Range Rover parked directly across from my building. All the windows are slightly tinted, so although the streetlights allow me to distinguish that someone is sitting in the driver's seat, I'm unable to make out if it's a male or female.

I've no idea how long the car has been there. Although I don't live in the worst of areas, it sticks out like a sore thumb in this neighbourhood, where the favoured cars tend to be Volkswagen Golf or Ford Fiesta. So I know it certainly wasn't there when I came home; I would have noticed it.

I turn the light off and stand peering through a small gap in the curtain simultaneously trying to avoid being seen. I'm wondering if I should call the police. But what would I say? I'd like to report a suspicious car parked outside my house. As far as I know that's not a crime.

I'm beginning to get a crick in my neck, so I decide to try and think nothing more of it and slide into bed. I prop my pillows up, sit back, get comfy, and open up my tablet to continue with the current murder mystery I'm reading. It's about a wife whose husband has faked his own death and is now stalking her, but no one will believe her.

I only manage to get through a few chapters when restless energy makes me unable to resist the curiosity niggling at me, and I get up to take another look out of the window.

The car is still there. It has now been thirty-five minutes since I first spotted it. I have a disturbing need to keep watching. But nothing significant is happening. Whoever it is, is just sitting there watching, waiting. But watching who? Waiting for what?

I wonder if the couple in the apartment above mine have spotted him. Maybe it's a woman. A jealous ex: there's no accounting for what a woman scorned is capable of. All logic goes out of the window. They become audacious, some even become neurotic in their quest for revenge.

"Jesus." The sudden shrill of my ring tone startles me, and my whole body slams against the wall. I put my hand on my chest as it rises and falls with my rapid breaths.

I grab the phone from the nightstand, cursing myself as I do so for not putting it on silent, and I sit on the bed.

When I notice the caller ID says private number, I'm not sure if it's the stranger outside that has me a little on edge, or the fright the sound of my phone gave me, but I hesitate for a fraction of a second before I answer.

I draw a shallow breath before I speak. "Hello."

"Do you need help getting to sleep?" His words are a breathy whisper, and my trepidation suddenly turns to excitement as my heart is now beating double time.

"Mark?"

"Are you in bed?"

"I'm sitting on the bed."

"Lie back and tell me what you're wearing." His voice is low and smooth, yet I can hear the hunger-filled desire as he says each word.

"I'm wearing my black satin cami and shorts."

Oh my God! Are we really going to do this? When I find myself doing as he asks, I realise that, yep, this is happening.

There's a slight groan on his side. "I want you to touch yourself, Lauren. Slide your hand down your stomach and slip it between your legs." His commanding tone makes it impossible for me to resist his instructions.

"If I were there now, how would you want me to take you?"

I can't answer, I'm too busy with my hand between my legs. I close my eyes to the sound of his deep voice lulling me into mentally imagining him here—I'm imagining it's his hand touching me, his fingers pleasuring me.

"You're too quiet, Lauren. I want to know what you're doing now. I want to hear your sexy moans."

"I'm touching myself. I'm imagining your hands fondling my breasts. Your fingers inside me."

"I'm getting hard just thinking about what you're doing to yourself right now. Which part of what I did to you when we fucked did you like the most, Lauren?"

"I liked the way you gave it to me hard and deep."

"And what about you? What did you like doing for me, Lauren?"

"I liked taking you in my mouth until you got off. I liked being able to bring you to your ecstasy." I also like the way he says my name; low, breathy, seductive.

"Do you want to know what I'm doing right now? I'm fisting myself. I'm pumping so hard that I'm going to come. I'm stroking myself, Lauren. I don't know what I want to do first, lick you dry or slam into you so hard that you beg me for more. There are so many things I want to do, and I'm going to do all of them, eventually. Do you want me as much as I want you? Do you want to be fucked as much as I want to fuck you? Do you want me to make you feel good?"

My hand is working so fast and hard that I can barely speak, and the words leave my lips in a quivering murmur. "Yes, I want all of those things."

"Are you ready for me, Lauren?"

Just as I'm close to the edge, he hangs up. "What the…?"

A mere few seconds later the phone rings again. I contemplate leaving it to finish what he started, but I have a sudden urge, maybe it's the desire flooding my body, longing for him, wanting him, that I answer the call.

"Let me in, Lauren."

I drop the phone, God knows where, and I get to the door in such a flash I'm not sure my feet even touch the ground.

I press the intercom buzzer to let him in and wait at my door, listening. I hear the main door close. I hear the faint sound of footsteps climbing the stairs to reach my apartment on the first floor. All the while, my heart is racing in anticipation, pounding hard from the excitement of seeing him.

As soon as he comes into view my heart misses a beat. He comes to a halt before me, mere inches from me that I want to reach out and touch him. I've only ever seen him in a suit, but he's proving he can rock a pair of jeans and a T-shirt. He must have gone home and changed after he left the bar.

As his eyes rake over my body, there's a fire smouldering within, an animalistic glint—he looks like the devil himself, and I'm entranced by the chocolate of his eyes as they roam my body.

I can feel the heat of a blush on my cheeks while he stands there getting an eyeful. He has a look of determination on his face when he steps over the threshold, tugs me away from the door, and kicks it shut, then pulls me into him. One hand is around my waist holding me to him, strong and firm, and in a tender moment the other hand smooths my hair, pushing a stray strand behind my ear.

Then all bets are off as he crushes his lips to mine, claiming them, caressing them, sending a swirl of yearning to the pit of my stomach.

He breaks from the kiss, and his gaze slowly drops from my eyes to my heaving breasts and back to my eyes in silent expectation. I nod and take his hand, leading him to my bedroom.

The lamp on the nightstand is casting a subtle glow in the room. The fragrant lavender oil that I drop onto my pillow every night to help me sleep floats in the air. The cosiness of my bed suddenly seems like the expanse of an ocean about to take me on a wave of gratification.

I lie on the bed, propping myself up on my elbows, and watch him as he takes a condom from his wallet and places it within reach on the nightstand.

He pulls the T-shirt out from the waist band of his jeans then tugs it over his head and tosses it to the floor. He kicks his shoes off, unzips his jeans, drops them, and shrugs them off purposefully.

He's standing before me, only his boxers between him and complete nakedness. My eyes immediately dart to his groin and the noticeable bulge, my core craving its attention. An internal cry of euphoria has me licking my lips as I watch him swiftly remove his boxers and discard them.

He lowers himself onto the bed, wastes no time as he pulls my cami over my head, then gently eases me down and straddles me. He proceeds to remove my shorts, the palms of his hands fiery hot against my sensitive skin. His warm lips kiss their way along my stomach, his tongue darting out to lick as he carves a path upwards, teasing my breasts until he reaches my lips.

"I don't know why I waited so long to call you."

"I'm glad you finally decided to."

He reaches for the condom and sheaths himself, no complaints from me, bearing in mind we've had our foreplay over the phone, then lowers his body to cover mine, and I delight in the sensation my nipples feel as his bare chest meets mine.

The moment he enters me is pure, explosive ecstasy. I succumb to the delirious feeling of being filled by him and wrap my legs around his waist as he goes deeper and harder. His pounding is relentless, God only knows where he gets his stamina.

Our bodies fit effortlessly together as we move in synchronisation. Only when we reach the height of passion, do we both strive for the final crescendo.

Succumbing to the strong whirlwind, he digs his hands into my hips before he thrusts one final time, letting out a satisfied groan.

I feel him pulsing inside me as his body shudders, and I bask in my own gratification as it rises inside me, ripping me apart, eliciting surrendering moans.

He collapses to the side of me, sweaty and breathless, and angles his gaze on me.

"Jesus, that was fucking incredible."

Feeling his penetrating gaze on me I turn my head to look at him. I can't help the satisfied smile that splays across my face as I notice his dark, intelligent eyes are filled with warmth and tenderness.

I come to the realisation that, for the first time in my life, I don't have to fake it with a guy—he's that good. And as I brazenly snuggle into him, to my surprise, he doesn't hesitate to welcome me into his arms.

"What do you like to do when you're not working?"

Amusement flickers in his eyes as they meet mine. "Apart from having sex. Hmm, that's a tough one."

"I'm serious. We've slept together twice, and I don't really know very much about you at all."

There's a deep sigh followed by a few seconds of silence before he answers. "I work hard and play hard."

"Isn't that rather cliché?"

"I like playing squash. I enjoy good food and fine wine. And I definitely enjoy fine women and great sex."

He rolls himself so that he's on top of me, holding my arms above my head, gently locking his hands around my wrists, pinning me down as he smiles at me playfully. "And you, Lauren, are one fine woman, and sex with you isn't just great, it's phenomenal."

Before I know it, his lips are on mine, kissing me hard, devouring me. When he raises his mouth from mine, he gazes at me, his eyes shining bright with undiluted pleasure. "You drive me fucking crazy. It makes me feel so out of control."

He places a gentle kiss on my forehead. He kisses the

tip of my nose. He bites my bottom lip. His tongue slides between the crevice of my breasts, then circles the nipple of each breast in turn, tantalizing each swollen bud.

"I'm going to kiss you all over. Then my tongue is going to give you the best oral you've ever had."

"Yes, please. Do it. I want you to do it now. I need you now."

He slides further down my body. He nibbles and licks my inner thigh. He uses his breath to warm my crotch then he does exactly what he said he would do as his tongue flicks and licks, swirls and delves. Up and down, side to side. I feel as though I'm being given a thousand lashes and it's like no other feeling I've ever had.

I scream his name in pure ecstasy, begging for him to stop, pleading with him to carry on. As the tension builds, I find myself writhing as I dig my fingers into his shoulders.

"Mark, I'm… it feels so… please…" I'm panting, breathless as I come down from my high as Mark slowly savours my wetness as it flows like warm honey.

When he slides his body up and aligns it with mine, there's a look of pure lust in his eyes as he leans in, and his moist lips take mine. I lie in the drowsy warmth of his arms as they pull me into him.

"What made you come here tonight? And more importantly, how did you know where I live?"

"You've been on my mind for the last few weeks, so I thought perhaps it was time to satisfy my unquenchable thirst for you."

"If you hadn't seen me at the bar tonight, would you have called me?"

"But I did call. That's all that really matters. After some coaxing, Jules gave me your address earlier at the bar."

"She's a sly one, she never mentioned it."

"Don't be too hard on her, I swore her to secrecy."

"I'm not angry. Far from it. If I'm honest, I'd given up on being with you like this again. I thought maybe I imagined how good things were the last time, or at the very least, I assumed it was all one sided."

"You didn't imagine it, and it wasn't."

I don't care that he waited three weeks to call me. And who knows if he ever would have if I hadn't bumped into him this evening.

All of that is immaterial. Like he said, the fact is he did call, and I'm now relishing the afterglow of the feeling you can only get after great sex, content to be thoroughly exhausted from fulfilment.

"Do you think we could make a habit of doing this? I know I'd like to see you again." *If you don't ask, you don't get.*

His brows arch, seemingly surprised that I would even broach the subject, as if I should know better.

"What exactly are you suggesting? I have a lot going on in my life right now. I don't have time to prioritise anything resembling a relationship."

He doesn't wait for my reply. He releases me from his embrace, slips out of bed, and goes to the bathroom to dispose of the condom. His reaction serves to tell me I've definitely asked for too much too soon. I flinch from the feeling of being rejected, not sure if I should feel sad, angry, disappointed. My shoulders slump, realising it's probably all three.

While Mark is in the bathroom I torture myself even more as I envisage having a relationship with him. I don't really know very much about him at all, apart from the fact that he's a very skilled lover and very considerate in bed, giving as much as he takes, that's for sure.

The fact that he's older, more mature, I think makes him decent boyfriend material. It's been a while since I've actually thought of being in a relationship myself. Ever since the stunt Andrew pulled, I've been reluctant to fully trust a man. My fling with the barman was exactly what I needed at the time, short, sweet, and sweaty.

Perhaps it's jealousy making me contemplate something bordering on "going steady" with him. I want him all to myself. I want him to be mine and only mine. I don't want him lowering his body over some other female and burying himself deep inside her. I don't want another woman giving him what I want to be giving him. I want to be the only one lying beneath him or on top of him. I want to be the only one to make him drown in his own pleasure, a pleasure only I give him.

Yep, I've definitely got it bad if I'm daydreaming of a happy ever after just because he knows where to stick it and how to use it. God forbid if Rachel could read my mind, she'd be planning my wedding.

I'm roused from my musings by the sound of his phone vibrating on the nightstand. I'm not an idiot, I know I shouldn't answer. But I do turn it face up to take a sneaky peek at the caller ID, because who would be calling at this time of the night? Another woman checking up on him no doubt.

Yep, that's what being cheated on and lied to will do to you. You question every little thing. You become paranoid. That's the result of finding out your boyfriend of six months actually has a wife. A fact you don't find out about until she turns up on your doorstep very early on a Saturday morning, when you're expecting to have a cosy lie-in with your so-called boyfriend, and she starts hurling abuse at you, waking up your neighbours in the process who in turn call the police to report a breach of the peace.

Nope, you couldn't make it up if you tried.

Of course he said he wanted to discuss things, explain. More likely he wanted to make excuses and empty promises. Even I'm not that stupid. Once a cheater always a cheater. We live and learn, and I've hopefully learnt to recognise the signs.

I glance at the screen. All it says is Rose. I replace it face down. Suddenly things start to register in my mind. He has a tattoo of a rose on the back of his hand. It doesn't take a genius to conclude that the two are related. But who is Rose? An ex-girlfriend? An ex-wife? A current girlfriend or wife? No. Jules would know if he had a wife. Note to self, ask Jules about Rose.

When he comes back, he grabs his clothes from the floor. I sit up, pulling the sheet across me, and watch him getting dressed while feeling a twinge of regret, not for what's happened, but for what is not going to happen. The fact that I even contemplated having anything meaningful means that I'd let my guard down. But Mark makes being with him so easy, and if there are any warning voices in my head, I've clearly chosen not to listen to them.

I chose to follow my desire and the extreme attraction I feel to this man, unrivalled by anything I've ever felt before, which should have made me cautious from the start.

We'd barely even spoken before. We'd only ever seen each other a handful of times before Jules and Adam's wedding, and despite being insanely attracted to him the moment I set eyes on him, at best we shared pleasantries.

This is only the second time we've had sex, yet I feel

this inexplicable strong pull towards him. It's most likely just lust, but it would have been nice to take things a little further and see if it could become something more.

I hide my disappointment, and not wanting any awkwardness, I'm about to ask him to just forget what I'd said earlier, but once he's dressed, he sits on the edge of the bed to put his shoes on. As he sits there, he rakes a hand though his hair and lets out a long breath as he peers at the ground. He seems to be churning something over in his mind, and it's a few seconds before he says anything at all.

He looks up at me, his darks eyes unfathomable, and I'm almost dreading what he's going to say as his mouth opens. I'm not a one-night stand virgin, and technically this is our second night, but it's still hard to hear the speech full of excuses.

"Okay, you win."

His choice of words is a little confusing, and my mind is working overtime to try and make sense of them. "What do I win exactly?"

Perhaps he can read my mind, or maybe it's my miserable attempt at trying to look nonchalant that has him adjust his position on the bed to get comfier. He lifts me into his lap and presses his lips to mine as if to silence me.

He toys with the silky locks of my hair for a moment before pushing them aside and palming my face with his hands. He seems to be studying me with piercing scrutiny, feature by feature.

Then his eyes gleam with mischievousness. "Why don't I take you out to dinner tomorrow evening."

I stare wordlessly for a moment before the corners of his mouth curve into a smile, instantly disarming me.

"I'd like that."

"Great, that's settled. I'll pick you up at seven." He pulls me off his lap, sets me down on the bed, and stands up. He grabs his wallet and phone. His brows rise in a flash of recognition when he has a quick glance at the screen, before slipping it in his pocket, and I stand to walk him to the door.

"You know you don't have to sneak out in the middle of the night. You could stay over."

There's a sudden pensiveness to his mood. "No, I can't. I need to get home." He leans in and places a soft kiss on my forehead. "I'll see you tomorrow."

Such is my excitement I Ignore the concerns my sixth sense is trying to arouse. I pretend I didn't notice the contented look on his face when he glanced at his phone. I skip merrily back to my bedroom and fall into bed in a giddy state of happiness, like a teen who's just had her first ever kiss from the boy she's been crushing on. I doubt very much I'll get any sleep tonight.

CHAPTER 5
Lauren

As excited as I am for tonight's date, I seem to have first-date jitters. It seems almost ridiculous that I'm wondering how I should greet him. Hug or no hug? Should we kiss in greeting? If we do, should it be on the cheek or on the lips? Anyone would think this is my first rodeo. I should be thankful for small mercies; at least the dilemma of whether or not we should sleep together on the first date is no longer something I need to worry about.

I want to wow him, so I've worn my slinkiest little black dress and my highest heels, which I almost trip in as I rush to answer the door.

When I open the door I see his six-foot frame standing there, looking drop-dead gorgeous. The heat of his eyes gives everything away as they linger over me. They're filled with a wild desire, sending a shiver of excitement through me, doing all kinds of thrilling things to my insides.

He's wearing a designer two-piece royal blue suit, white shirt sans tie, the top two buttons undone giving me a glimpse of flesh, teasing me with the knowledge of the muscles that lie beneath. His strong, broad shoulders remind me of his strength and stamina. It all just makes me want to give in now, offer myself up to him, let him have his wicked way with me and bare his children.

His stare is bold as his eyes continue to openly roam my body, seductively assessing me from head to toe, then letting his gaze drift to my face.

"Will I do?" I ask.

His smile grows wider until it's a full-blown grin, beaming his approval. He leans in; his lips brush against my ear, raising goosebumps across the back of my neck. "You'll do very nicely." His lips place a soft kiss on mine.

After I lock up, he puts his hand on the small of my back as we make our way out of the building to his sleek black Range Rover with its personalised number plate, MT 1. He guides me to the passenger side and opens the door for me.

It's another reminder of that arsehole of a so-called boyfriend and his shortcomings. Because Andrew never opened doors for me. At the time I wasn't upset or offended; in fact, I tend to feel that women who expect that sort of treatment are high maintenance, spoiled, and entitled. But when Mark does it, he somehow makes me feel special.

Once we're comfortably ensconced inside and seatbelts are buckled, the engine purrs into life and we speed off.

When we arrive at the swanky restaurant in central London, I open my door, but in true prince charming fashion, before I can make another move, Mark is out of the car and on my side offering his hand as I step out.

The restaurant he's chosen serves a mix of British comfort food and modern European dishes. As we're escorted to our table, I take in the modern décor and furnishings, which create a relaxing space.

Mark is walking with confidence. Shoulders back, head up. His mere presence commands your attention, but he seems oblivious to the fact that all eyes are probably on him as he has a hand firmly on my waist, keeping me near to him so he can guide me to our table.

Conversation flows effortlessly. I learn that he's known Adam for ten years, having met when Adam availed himself of Mark's legal services. He lives in Hampstead. Doesn't think twice about working all hours to get the job done. And as we've already established, he works hard and plays hard. Hard being the operative word.

"What about you? Tell me about the advertising world."

"Things have picked up since Jules left. I think it was a wake-up call for the company. They've realised they need to switch things up if they want to keep their staff. We've started to get some interesting clients. One of our recent signings and one of my current campaigns is for a dildo company."

His eruption of laughter causes the whole restaurant to stop and stare. He composes himself, then raises his eyebrows questioningly.

"Okay, I know your dying to ask me. Go ahead."

"Tell me, do you take your work home with you?"

Externally I feign being over the tiresome one-liners, but internally, I delight in his silly side. "Sometimes. This particular campaign requires that I fully immerse myself into the sampling of the product to appreciate what it can do. It all makes for a successful campaign." I bite the inside of my cheek to try and keep a straight face.

His smile has a spark of eroticism as he reaches across the table and traces his fingers sensuously over my bare arm, enough to tease and titillate. But it's his words that excite me as they stimulate my libido.

"Perhaps that's something we can do together. I'm all for performance testing, seeing how things compare to the real thing. We can rate hardness. Take measurements. Durability is important, curve, fitting, and robustness. But I'd say the most important requirement is intensity. I'm more than happy to offer my services."

There's something delightfully attractive in his humour. But before I can answer, his phone rings softly, and he takes it from the pocket of his suit jacket. He glances at the screen, and I notice how his demeanour changes from being playfully seductive to thoughtful, and his expression is one of tenderness as his mouth curves for a brief second and his eyes seem to be filled with happiness.

"Excuse me while I take this. Hello. No, I'm out at dinner."

He listens to whoever is on the other end.

"Okay, I'll be home soon. We'll talk about it then." He hangs up, lets out a sigh before focusing back on me.

"Is everything okay?"

"I'm afraid something has come up. We're going to have to cut our evening short."

"Sure. Is there a problem?" I try digging but my shovel obviously isn't up for the challenge, as he doesn't answer that particular question, leading me to the conclusion that it's something personal. *Is he seeing someone else? Going home to who?* I'm no Columbo, so I'll ride the wave until something concrete presents itself.

He plasters a grin on his face. "Let's order dessert."

We both order the chocolate souffle. Each mouthful melts on my tongue, and I can't help slowly licking the back of my spoon with each rich, velvety, spoonful of chocolate.

One brow arches in amusement as he watches me. "Are you enjoying that?"

I nod and lick my lips as I finish the last of the souffle and put the spoon down. "Uh-huh. So delicious."

His eyes openly fall from mine to my lips, and further down to my breasts. Their eagerness arousing me. He licks his own lips as he casually teases me. "I think I'd best get you home before I'm tempted to ravage you right here."

He drops me at my apartment building and walks me to the main entrance. "I had a great time. Thank you for dinner," I say.

He moves closer until there is no space between us. His fingers trail down my temple. His hand brushes the hair from my shoulder, then lightly grips my neck as his lips slowly descend, smothering mine. I place my hands on his biceps, and I get the added thrill of feeling his hard muscles beneath my fingertips. He doesn't need to force my lips apart, they do so willingly. His lips are warm and moist, strong, and hard, but the kiss is gentle. Its deliciousness singing through my veins, causing soft moans to escape from my lips.

As he pulls away, I breathe lightly between parted lips. My heart pounds; my legs tremble from the eager response of his kiss, of his touch.

There's a moment's silence as his dark eyes study my face, and I attempt to make sense of the play of emotions from his expression.

Is it satisfaction—smug delight at knowing he's unleashed this intense need for him and the pleasures he bestows?

Biting my bottom lip, and as casually as I can manage

to sound, I say the words tentatively, as if testing the waters.

"So, you'll call me?"

His brows rise in surprise, and he beams a smile at me, full of humour, and in case I'm in any doubt, his reply brings clarity. "What the fuck do you think?"

CHAPTER 6
Mark

Of course I meant it when I said I would call her. And it's a great ego boost to know she was eager to see me again.

What's disturbing and taken me completely by surprise is the fact that despite it being less than twenty-four hours since I last saw her, I feel almost desperate to be see her. There's an urgency to be with her again. How is it even possible? I barely know her. But I want to get to know her. That's the overwhelming effect she has on me that no other woman has had.

I leave my office informing my PA that I'm going for an early lunch and may be back a little later than the requisite hour. I am the boss, after all.

I take a cab from Mayfair to Covent Garden, the journey taking longer than necessary because of the London traffic. Stop start. Stop start. It seems that every single traffic light on our route turns red as we approach, just to piss me off, making me impatient. I just want to fucking be there already. I should have taken the underground.

When I do finally arrive, I make my way through the lobby to the bank of three lifts. I search the list of companies displayed on the brass plaque fixed to the wall and make my way up to the third floor.

When I step out, I approach the reception desk whilst looking around me. I'm intrigued to be in her place of work, enthusiastic to see this side of her.

The receptionist's voice grabs my attention. "May I help you."

As I'm about to ask to see Lauren, I spot Rachel walking across the open-plan office. She does a double take when she sees me, her eyes wide in surprise. She immediately starts to walk towards me.

"It's okay, Kim. I've got this. Hey, Mark." She kisses me on the cheek. "How are things with you?"

"Good. Great in fact."

"I take it you're here to see Lauren. Follow me."

I'm not sure whether or not it's my imagination, but there seems to be a distinct air of cheerfulness and satisfaction in her manner as she escorts me to Lauren's desk. I do as I'm told and follow her. There are some people still at their desks despite it being lunch time. I'm all for dedication to your work.

We turn the corner to where there are three more desks, and I immediately spot Lauren hunched over hers, studying the screen of her laptop.

"Hey, Lauren. You have a visitor."

She looks up from the screen, her brows drawn together. Then she takes off her glasses. How did I not know she wears glasses? As soon as she does so, a wide smile permeates her face, reaching her eyes as they gleam with surprise.

"I'll leave you two to it. Great to see you, Mark."

She disappears before I can say anything else as I'm too enamoured by the pleasing sight before me.

"What are you doing here?"

I approach her desk. "I thought perhaps I could take you to lunch."

"Oh. I've just had a sandwich. I wasn't going to go out for lunch today. Too busy, you know how it is."

Fuck. Is she shooting me down? I persevere, using all my charm and determination. "I'm sure you can spare half an hour or so. Since it's not raining, how about we make the most of it and go for a walk around Covent Garden Piazza?"

She's biting her bottom lip, mulling over my suggestion. "I am really busy. But I guess I can take a break for an hour. I'll just grab my jacket."

We spend twenty minutes walking around the Piazza, stopping briefly to watch the street entertainers, before I suggest we sit and have a coffee.

"I didn't know you wore glasses."

She laughs as she places her cup down on its saucer. "It's not generally a great conversation starter. I wear them for reading. It's not something I usually disclose until things become serious with a guy. You know, meet-the-parents kind of serious."

"Are you making fun of my dialogue?" I find her teasing enchanting. In fact, everything about her has me spellbound. From her laughter to her positivity. She talks enthusiastically about her work and her friends. She seems to give everything her all. She's certainly a breath of fresh air. So different from the usual women I hook up with, who usually want constant affirmation as to their looks or where I think the *relationship* is going. Then I have to deal with their sulkiness when I casually remind them we're not in a relationship.

"Yep. Just a little. Do you know that your eyes narrow

when you're ruffled?"

"They do not," I say feigning wounded pride. "And I'm not ruffled. I'm extremely delighted that I'm able to assist in providing you with your afternoon entertainment."

She gives a slight shake of her head as she smiles at me. Her glowing eyes display her enjoyment. "To what do I owe this unexpected lunch date?"

"I was at a loose end. No meetings this afternoon."

"Hmm, you're not going to admit it's because you were desperate to see me after our date last night."

"Would it surprise you if I did admit it?"

There's a sly smirk as she leans in and rests a hand on my thigh. That gesture alone gives me palpitations. And before I know it, I feel the delicious sensation of her lips on mine. It's a quick soft kiss, very suitable for public consumption, but the mere thrill of it has my cock throbbing and craving to be inside of her.

"How about playing hooky? I can think of an activity or two we can do back at my place."

She shakes her head disbelievingly and smiles in amusement. "As an employer and a lawyer aren't you supposed to be the epitome of law-abiding strait-laced?"

"As the boss I can more or less do as I please, and you'd be surprised what I can get away with."

"So what you're suggesting is that I skip work for the rest of the day to spend it with you, playing games, which no doubt involve us being horizontal?"

"I had in mind something different, exploratory."

She draws her bottom lip in between her teeth as she contemplates what I've just said. "Are you hinting at wanting to introduce your Dom tendencies into the bedroom?"

"There's no pulling the wool over your eyes, maybe a

blindfold?"

"I'll give you ten out of ten for effort, but it's going to be a hard no, unfortunately."

Yep. Definitely hard. "You can't blame a guy for trying."

She leans in and lowers her voice. There's a complete look of enthrallment in her eyes. "Maybe you haven't tried hard enough in your endeavours."

Is it any wonder there's something about this woman that has me coming back for more? Of course I've had sex with the same woman more than once. But I've never craved to be buried deep inside a woman the way I do Lauren. I've never counted the days before I'm able to fuck the same woman again. I get hard just thinking about getting her naked and having her shapely body snuggled against mine, two becoming one. It's more than a mild interest. It feels much more than sexual desire. I actually want to be with her, in her presence, regardless of whether we have sex or not. It's a feeling I've never had before. I'm in unchartered waters—heading into dangerous territory.

I am so fucked.

CHAPTER 7
Lauren

After our impromptu lunch date, Mark remained true to his word and called me over the following week. But the plans we made were then cancelled by him. No explanation given. I get it. It's not the first time a guy has tried to play it cool. But I haven't heard from him for a few days. Maybe I imagined how off the charts it was. Maybe the way he makes me feel inside, bringing my senses to life, is all in my imagination. Either way, I want to see him again, and my instinct tells me it's just a matter of time. Although it's not one of my strong points, for a man like him, I can exercise patience.

My patience pays off, and we finally go on another date, two weeks after our last. We visit an exhibition of Fabergé craftsmanship at The Victoria and Albert Museum in Kensington.

As we walk around viewing exhibits, he takes hold of my hand, something that surprises me since he doesn't seem one for romantic gestures. I thought showing up unexpectedly to take me to lunch was as romantic as he would get.

But whilst his sweet, intoxicating scent fills me with

excitement, and being with him makes my pulse race, makes my heart flutter, his nearness makes my whole body quiver; I need to pay attention to the signs staring me in the face.

It's not only the cancelled dates with no explanation, although there's clearly a pattern emerging. It's always the same days of the week and every other weekend. It's baffling. The signs are also there as we walk around the museum. The furtive glance at his phone. Letting go of my hand and falling behind with his constant need to check for messages or missed calls. This all leads to him being distracted. What is that all about?

It can only add up to one thing. Another woman. My mind goes back to the caller ID on his phone *Rose.* But despite my suspicions, each time I'm with him I fall for him a little more. So I've convinced myself I'm imagining it. I've convinced myself that I'm being paranoid. I've told myself that because Andrew is a lying, cheating scumbag, one bad apple doesn't make the whole bunch bad.

Am I being naïve or just plain stupid because of the great sex he so skilfully supplies? This is a two-way street. As long as we're both getting what we want, what's the harm?

Once our tour of the museum is over, we sit in an Italian restaurant in Knightsbridge to have a late lunch. That's when he goes one step further and gets up to leave from the table in order to take a call. I'll give him points for not actually leaving the restaurant; he merely moves a short distance away, standing near the door to the kitchen area, talking low and discreetly. Turning his back to me when he notices me watching him.

When he gets back to the table, the inward questions come thick and fast, making me determined to at least try and extract some kind of acceptance from him that his behaviour is not only curious, but unacceptable.

He sits down and places the napkin on his lap. "Sorry about that."

"Problems at work?" It's a Saturday, so technically, I doubt this is true. But I'm giving him an opportunity—an opening to come clean—divulge some information. Give me something that I can deem acceptable. Something to ease the thoughts in the back of my mind and that he's not seeing another woman.

He hesitates just a fraction, but then with an easy confidence and without flinching, he says, "Nope. Just personal stuff." He doesn't look at me as he speaks, he fiddles with the cutlery, then takes a sip of his wine.

Shifty behaviour if ever I saw it.

I sit up straight, lace my fingers together, and rest my forearms on the table as I lean in slightly. With my pulse pounding, steadfast in my determination, I do what I know I have to do. End this before we, or should I say I, devote any more time and emotion. I've already fallen for him. End it before I have my heart broken into a million pieces.

"Listen, Mark, if you're seeing someone else, then I'm sorry to say that this, we, has to stop."

He becomes instantly focused on me, seemingly surprised by what I've just said. He lets out a long sigh.

"Are you married? Is that it?" Although I already know the answer. I asked Jules, and it was an emphatic no. But I want to get him to open up a little. I want him to know he doesn't have to hide anything from me. He can trust me.

"I'm not married."

"Then what? Is it a girlfriend—friend with benefits?"

If it's not work related, what else can it be other than

another woman? I get it. He's drop-dead gorgeous. What woman wouldn't want to be in his company or in his bed.

"As I've already said, it's personal. It has nothing to do with you or us. It's not you, it's me."

I unconsciously slam a hand on the table. "Oh my God! Did you just say that? I'm not stupid, Mark. Please don't treat me as if I am."

He shows no reaction to my outburst other than to look at me, giving me a penetrating stare, his eyes holding mine, his voice low and commanding. "Please keep your voice down. For the record, I do not think you're stupid, and I apologise if you feel that I'm treating you as if you are. That is not my intention."

I actually feel deflated now, but I hide it. I know we haven't been seeing each other very long. This is only our second official date, but why is he so secretive about his personal life? He's keeping me at arm's length. Why? There are too many unanswered questions. Sure the only logical reason is that there is another woman. I have a sneaky suspicion it's all to do with Rose. Who is she? Maybe a dependant ex-wife? I believe him when he says he's not married, but married or not, I won't be the other woman, not again, especially knowingly.

I respond matter-of-factly. Deciding not to hide my frustration. "Right. Okay." I proceed to tuck into my spaghetti, twisting it around my fork before shoving it in my mouth.

A shadow of frustration flits across his face as he lets out a long slow breath. "Lauren, we've known each other, what? All of five minutes. Let's not jump ahead of ourselves. Let's take it for what it is. Let's enjoy each other. There's no need to charge full steam ahead as if we're on a freight train. Let's see how long our journey is and where it takes us. If things progress, then we can start divulging the personal things about ourselves." He pushes a piece of lasagne onto his fork and into his mouth.

I swallow my food, put my fork down, and stare in bewilderment. Does that mean he's open to us being more than just about the sex? I'm wondering what on earth I've gotten myself into. Wondering why I'm going to accept what he says when I should know better. As great as it is, as good as he is, surely it's crazy to base my decision purely on the sex and how he makes me feel.

He seems oblivious to my inner turmoil as he praises the restaurant. As if his word is the last word on the matter. "The food here is great, don't you think? You really should try the tiramisu for dessert. It's the best I've ever had."

When his phone rings again quietly in his jacket pocket my eyes are fixated on his. I look at him hopefully, willing him not to answer, but he does. This time he has the decency to remain seated as he answers, I guess that's progress. He listens for a few seconds before speaking.

"I'll be there in an hour." And he hangs up.

As curious as I am, I don't even bother to question him because I know he'll just dodge my questions. I make the most of what's left of our lunch, and by five o'clock we're in a taxi heading home.

When we come to a stop at my apartment building, he gets out first and holds the cab door open for me.

As he walks me to the main door, his hands are warm and strong as they grasp mine. "I had a great time today," he says.

I bend my head, looking down at our interlaced fingers. "Me too."

"So, we can do it again very soon?"

"I guess so, when you can make time for me."

A smile ruffles his mouth as his response to my little dig is to release my hands and cup my face, leaning in, claiming my mouth, crushing his lips to mine. His kiss is almost punishing. His tongue exploring and swirling. His kiss is intoxicating, passionate, persuasive. I shamelessly kiss him back hungrily, desperately. Not wanting it to end, but it does.

As he pulls away, I'm left almost breathless, drawing in the air between my parted lips.

"I have a dinner, a work thing, perhaps you could be my date. Although I should warn you that you may find it a bore."

"If I'm free. When is it?"

"Next week. Wednesday evening. I'll pick you up at six."

"Sure, okay. I can do that."

He's starts to walk to the waiting cab but stops midstride and turns, his words are said with a detached calm.

"Lauren, I don't want to push you into anything. We're having fun. I don't have time to cultivate a relationship. I'm not a flowers and chocolates kind of guy."

Well that's a kick in the teeth. I have my share of trust issues since Andrew. I readily hold my hands up to that. So I'm not entirely sure why the honesty of his words cut close to the bone, but they bring with them a feeling of humiliation. It feels as though he's just slapped me across the face, and I'm angry at myself for feeling disappointed, for getting my hopes up only to have them dashed when I should know better.

"What makes you think I'm a flowers and chocolates kind of girl?"

"I just want us to be on the same page."

Not wanting him to know that the depth of my feelings has already gone from lounging in the shallow end to jumping off at the deep end, I resolve to show him he's not the only one not looking for a commitment, even if I am kidding myself. I meet his stare straight on. His eyes betray him as they smoulder with an intensity and an eagerness to hear what I have to say.

"I'm not looking for a long-term commitment, Mark. I just don't want to be one of many. I don't want you to be taking another woman's calls when you're with me. And I certainly don't want you having sex with other women while you're fucking me. I don't think that's too much to ask of someone I'm having sex with. So if we're not on the same page in that regard, then we should call it quits now."

There's a gleam in his eyes, almost as if he's proud of my steadfastness, as we look at each other and smile in acknowledgement of the clarity that's been brought to the situation.

He walks back towards me, leans in, unable to stifle the need to smile, a trace of triumph in his voice. "Well, now that we've settled that, I'll see you on Wednesday. And I promise that before the night is over, you're going to be drowned in your own ecstasy as I fuck you into oblivion."

Hiding my euphoria and barely able to stop the rush of sheer delight at his words, I bask in his promise. "You always have to have the last word."

CHAPTER 8

Lauren

When we arrive at the Michelin-starred restaurant, we're immediately shown to our table, where I see two other couples are seated already.

Although I would have preferred to have him to myself, I'm taking it as a compliment that he would want me at his side for a work-related dinner.

The two men stand to greet us, and Mark does the introductions. Both women are glamourous. Both blondes, both with red manicured fingernails, and no doubt both vying for the spot of poster girl for De Beers, considering the amount of diamonds on display.

I discreetly fiddle with my modest, studded Tiffany diamond earrings, a twenty-first birthday present from my mum.

One couple appear older, in their late sixties I'd guess. The other couple are a mix. He looks older, late fifties, she looks in her forties, unless she has a good plastic surgeon. But I do notice the slight quirk of a brow when Mark introduces me simply as Lauren, which confirms there's no Botox. I suspect, just like me, she's wondering what exactly our relationship is.

I can't say that I'm not a little disappointed at how he's introduced me. For some reason I was hoping he would say "This is Lauren, my girlfriend" but I manage to keep any evidence of my feelings internal.

Mark pulls out my chair for me. It's a round table, and I'm seated between him and Susanna, the eyebrow lady.

The wine is flowing freely, and she seems to be taking full advantage. She turns to me with a crooked smile, her words slightly slurred.

"You look... nice."

"Thank you."

"Is that dress Prada? I don't recognise it. Must be last season."

She's just met me. She knows nothing about me. Why is she being bitchy towards me? Instead, I choose to ignore her catty comments.

"Actually, it's Zara."

"I don't know that designer."

"It's high street fashion." I could mention to her that she looks like a real-life blow-up doll with her pumped-up, pouty lips and breast implants, but I don't.

"Do you Live in London?" she asks.

I answer enthusiastically, pleased that her frostiness appears to be thawing, and she seems to be a little more friendly. "Yes, I'm a born and bred Londoner. I live and work here."

Her voice rises in surprise. "You work?"

I decide to try to remain polite and ignore her surprised reaction. "What about you? What do you do?" I'm not sure what I've said, perhaps it's the way I've said it, but she laughs, and it isn't a jovial laugh, it feels almost as if she's mocking me.

It's now very clear by her startled reaction that she's a trophy wife. The word work isn't even in her vocabulary. But perhaps I'm being too harsh, too quick to judge her life choices without knowing her story. So I ignore her patronizing comments and plough on in an attempt to make polite conversation. But I realise I'm being too optimistic when she continues with her charge, coming in for the attack from another angle.

"Mark, darling," she says, interrupting his conversation with the others. "Does Lauren work for you? If you needed a date you should have said. Christina would love to see you again. Only yesterday she was telling me in great detail how much fun the two of you had."

My mouth drops open, stunned by her bluntness. I want to tear into her. Give her a piece of my mind. But I quickly clamp my mouth shut. I'm here to support Mark. I don't want to do anything to embarrass him in front of his clients. I'll just have to take the higher ground and let this one go.

Mark turns to her as the table falls silent. His annoyance transparent as he gives her a seething look, his voice heavy with sarcasm.

"Sorry to disappoint you, Susanna, but Lauren isn't a lawyer, she's in advertising. She's very, very good at what she does." As he glances at me he winks, making it clear that his double entendre is deliberate.

"You really ought to ask her about it, you may learn a thing or two. Lauren enjoys her work. She's worked hard to make a success of her career. She has absolutely no aspirations to be anyone's trophy, let alone be kept by a man. That's one of the many things I like about her, her independence."

While I'm secretly beaming inside at how proud he is

of my achievements, her mouth tightens in frustration at being shot down.

"Well said, old chap," says the older husband of the other woman, Helen. "And is the delightful Lauren the one that's going to pin you down once and for all?"

I look at him hopefully, his expression like a mask of stone, giving nothing away. I wait with bated breath for his reply, but it doesn't come. He simply indicates with a motion of his hand that the interrupted discussion about the division of assets should continue.

I try to angle myself so that I can perhaps join in with Mark's conversation, anything to avoid Susanna, but she's caught me again.

"Tell me, Lauren, how did you and Mark meet?"

It's blatantly clear by now that Susanna is the bitch from hell, and for some inexplicable reason, she's determined to rattle my cage and rub me up the wrong way. Since I'm not in the mood to fake interest in making conversation with her, I decide to keep my answer short and sweet so as not to have to engage any longer than necessary with her.

"My best friend recently married a friend of his."

Her brows rise again in recognition, and her voice is suddenly filled with a rasp of interest and excitement. "Oh, do you mean Adam Foster?"

I'm taken aback by her knowledge. So, since I now have something to talk about with a woman that I have absolutely nothing in common with, I answer her.

"Yes, do you know him?"

She takes another mouthful of wine and places the almost empty glass down, silently instructing her husband to top up her glass with a gesture of her hand.

He leans in. "Darling, don't you think you've had

enough?"

She seems incensed by this. Glaring at him, her stare alone causes tension as the silence looms between them. I notice his Adam's apple bob as he swallows before picking up the bottle and refilling her glass.

She turns to me, all fake smiles and white teeth, picking up where we left off. "Of course I know Adam Foster. I'm sure you can tell by my accent I'm an American. Everyone knows Adam Foster. His reputation precedes him. Do you know Oliver King?"

"No, I haven't met him. I believe he lives in New York."

"Did you know, before Oliver King got married they were known as the Three Amigos? They would spend summers in the Hamptons partying. It was quite something. They would leave a trail of broken hearts behind them. Oliver King and Adam Foster were bestowed with the title of being the most eligible bachelors on the East Coast. And as for Mark Taylor, well, he was, is, the quintessentially, very desirable, British Gent." She lowers her voice and leans in so as not to be overheard. "I'm hoping you're going to tell me it's just a cruel rumour, and that in fact, he's not such a gentleman."

I clear my throat. She's finally managed to shock me, not an easy feat. "Erm, I wouldn't know." I can't believe she's asking me these things with her husband sitting right there. I'm not about to discuss the ins and outs of mine and Mark's relationship, sexual or otherwise.

But my non-response doesn't deter her. "It's just that many have tried and failed to tie Mark Taylor down. How long have you been sleeping together? Are the rumours about his prowess true? Oh dear, have I put you on the spot. From what Christina tells me, he's very generously endowed, and he knows his way around the female body.

She says she came multiple times in one night. Are you exclusive? Are you hoping it's serious? Mark Taylor doesn't do serious! I am curious to know how you're managing to keep his interest. How much younger than him are you?"

Give me strength. She hasn't even taken a breath. I decide that now is as good a time as any to go to the loo. "Would you excuse me." I place my napkin on the table, and such is my infuriation, I rise from my chair as if propelled by an explosive force, the legs of my chair scraping along the tiled floor as Mark turns in his seat and grabs my wrist.

"Are you okay?" He looks up at me with eyes full on concern as they search mine for answers.

"I'm just off the ladies' room." I kiss him on the lips in appreciation of his concern and also to annoy Susanna.

After I wash my hands, I'm touching up my lipstick when trophy wife number two enters. She gently places a hand on my shoulder, and I look up to see her reflection in the mirror as she stands beside me.

"Lauren, don't take anything Susanna says to heart. She's just jealous."

I twist my lipstick closed and drop it into my clutch bag and turn to face her. Her words have made me curious, and I stare at her for a moment, baffled. "What has she got to be jealous about?"

"What she has failed to tell you, or should I say admit, is that she had her eye on Mark a while back. If truth be known she had her eye on Adam Foster too."

I take a moment to digest what she's just told me. An image of Susanna making a play for Mark comes to the forefront of my mind and gives me a shiver. Then I smile, savouring the satisfaction that I'm getting to enjoy something she wanted.

"I suppose that would explain it, then. But she seems happy dripping in diamonds and spending her days pampering herself. I'm not wrong am I? That's all she does."

"Yes, but have you taken a look at the old coot she has to sleep with to get those things?"

"Silly me, I just assumed when two people got married they loved each other."

Clearly something I've said amuses her, and her gentle laughter ripples through the air. "Oh, my dear, she's not married to him. She's working on becoming wife number four. Wife number three is at home in Chelsea, probably with her yoga instructor keeping her company."

The penny has finally dropped. "I see."

"And before you ask, yes, that is my husband. He may be a crotchety old thing, but he's my crotchety old thing."

Our burst of laughter floats through the air, and we only manage to calm ourselves down when someone enters the ladies' room. They become awkward and fix us with a bewildered stare. I give a courteous smile to our intruder, grab my bag, and follow Helen back to our table. Our laughter has thankfully diminished by the time we re-join the others.

When I sit down Mark turns to me, places a hand on my thigh and squeezes. He leans in and whispers in my ear. "Are you sure you're okay? I know she's a bitch. Try to ignore her."

I nod as his reassuring words and his touch, along with what I've just learned from Helen, goes some way towards alleviating my frustrations over Susanna.

His voice has a velvety edge to it as he whispers his version of sweet nothings. "I know you're probably bored to death, but I'll make it up to you when I get you home. That's a promise."

That gains him a smile of approval so wide that he laughs before turning his attention back to the others.

Susanna leans in on my other side. She lowers her voice, and knowing full well the answer to her own question, delights in asking, "Have you met Rose?"

***

I slide the key in the lock and open the door for us to enter. Mark closes the door behind him and follows me to the kitchen.

"Tea or coffee?" I ask.

He's leaning casually against the countertop. "Hmm, asking me up for a nightcap wasn't a metaphor?"

"Nope." Thankfully, I'm able to stifle my laugh.

He playfully raises one brow. "I'll have tea, then."

He watches me as I fill the kettle, take two mugs from the cupboard, and being too lazy to bother with a pot, I drop a tea bag in each. "That was a very interesting group of people."

He lets out a throaty laugh. "Your choice of words is very generous."

"If you don't really like these people, what exactly was tonight in aid of?"

"Do you like all the products or clients you have to work with?"

I think about it for a second or two. My most recent campaign has been the most exciting in a long time. "No, not always, but I have to suck it up and do the best job I can."

"It's not any different for me, even if I am the boss. I have a law firm that employs over a hundred people, from lawyers, trainees, admin staff. If I pick and choose which clients to act for based on who I like, I wouldn't be in business for very long, and the people I employ would be out of a job."

I nod in acknowledgment and understanding. "What about Susanna? She ought to come with a warning label. What's the story there?"

"Jack Waller has a roving eye and likes the ladies. We're in the process of settling the prenup with the current wife before he signs another with the next."

"That would be the delectable Susanna, I take it. Helen mentioned her past interest in you. And who is Christina? Should I be jealous?"

"Christina is a friend of Susanna's. We had one night together. Something she would like to repeat. Something I do not wish to revisit. With regard to Susanna, I would rather not be reminded of her stalkerish behaviour. And before you ask, no, I've never had sex with her. I'd been dodging that woman for two years before she set her sights on Jack Waller. Thankfully someone came along with a bigger bank balance. And don't let all the Botox and surgery fool you. She's at least ten years older than me."

I burst out laughing.

"What's so funny?"

"I'm sorry, I can't help it. It's the thought of you and her together. She is so not your type."

He straightens himself and moves close to me, wraps his arms around my waist, and holds me tightly. "And you would know all about my type?"

"I think I've got a good handle on it."

"Maybe I should keep you around to ward off unwanted attention from the likes of Susanna."

"Is that the only reason you want to keep me around?" I try to wriggle free as the kettle comes to a boil, but he keeps a tight hold of me.

He nuzzles my hair. "Let's forget about the tea."

He sweeps me up into the cradle of his arms and carries me to the bedroom. As he gently places me on the bed, his body hovers above mine. I don't want to be blinded by my attraction to him. I don't want to have my head buried in the sand. Past experience has taught me not to ignore something that's playing on my mind. If it's such a secret how does Susanna know about Rose? Why hasn't Jules mentioned her?

Torn between wanting to find out more about Rose and not wanting to know anything in case it spoils this, I bite my bottom lip as I prepare myself to ask the dreaded question. I need to know. Maybe she's his ninety-year-old grandmother and the tattoo is just a loving tribute, and all my worries are misplaced.

As his hands sensuously explore, he whispers, his hot breath against my ear. "So goddam sexy. You turn me on so much. Do I make you feel as good as you make me feel?"

It's a rhetorical question because he doesn't wait for a reply. But as he's about to swoop down and pepper kisses all over my body I somehow decide now is the time not to falter in my determination. Now is the time to broach the subject.

"Who is Rose?"

He stops suddenly and props himself up on his forearms at each side of my head. Clearly surprised at what I've asked, he's looking down at me, and as our eyes meet, he draws his lips in as he seems to be studying me thoughtfully.

As I stare back, aware of his scrutiny, I blink nervously, which seems to interrupt his thoughts and his expression becomes one of complete concern, and the gentle tone of his voice is filled with seriousness. "I promise you don't need to worry about that."

"But—"

He silences me with his mouth. His lips capturing mine. His thrusting tongue demanding entry.

His kisses leave me weak and confused. So much so that all my thoughts of Rose are spinning away as I believe in his promises. I'm all too aware of the hardness brushing against my thigh and our eagerness has us scrambling to remove our clothes.

I do what any normal red-blooded female would do, I succumb to the pleasure only a skilful lover can bestow.

CHAPTER 9
Lauren

If I had known what the day ahead had in store for me, I would most likely have stayed in bed.

This morning the postman must have had an extra bowl of granola giving him added fuel, because unlike every other day, today my post arrives before I leave for work. I scoop up the two nondescript envelopes from the mat as I leave and shove them into my tote.

It isn't until lunch time, while I'm sitting at my desk having my tuna-mayo sandwich, that I remember the letters.

I dig them out of my bag and open the first, which turns out to be notification for the renewal of my home insurance. It's the second letter that has me hyperventilating and almost choking on my lunch. I reach for my bottled water and take small sips.

I frantically scrutinize the document to make sure I haven't misunderstood the contents, which only confirms the accuracy of my first interpretation.

I grab my phone and text Rachel to meet me in the loos. I rush to my feet and scurry through the open-plan office towards the door of the ladies' room.

Rachel is there before me and is immediately alerted that something is wrong by the fact that my breath has stalled, and I'm unable to speak. My trembling hands are waving the piece of paper in front of her. She grabs it from me, and I watch her eyes dart back and forth as she peruses the document. I know the exact moment she gets to the juicy part because her eyes freeze wide.

I rub my sweaty palms on my dress as I watch her. After a few minutes of pacing back and forth while she thinks, she finally stills herself and speaks. "This has got to be some kind of joke. What possible reason would she have to do this? It doesn't make sense."

This is certainly no laughing matter, but that's what I do. I break out into nervous, hysterical laughter. It's either that or scream from the frustration of it all.

Rachel glares at me, her face scrunched up with worry. "Why are you laughing?"

"Because if I don't, I'll bloody end up crying." I manage to calm myself down by focusing on Rachel's now relaxed and gentle tone.

She moves closer to me and places a hand on my arm. "Here's what we're going to do. You're going to call Mark —"

My voice rises in surprise at her suggestion as I shake my head in opposition to the mere thought of it. "Why the hell would I call him? He's the last person I would want to tell."

Over the course of the last two weeks I've seen Mark once. I don't know why he makes plans if he knows full well he's going to cancel. And to really add insult to injury, when he did cancel, he did it via text. I thought about what my response should be. There's the "Okay, thanks for letting me know" or "Sure, let me know when you want to reschedule." "Seriously, you're cancelling again?" is another option. Eventually, I decided not to reply at all.

Most women would at this point be wondering if they're pretty enough. They would ask if they're slim enough. Maybe he doesn't like their mannerisms or the way they talk. Maybe they're not good enough in bed? All of these things add pressure. So when a guy cancels a date without, in your mind, a rational explanation, it can drive you insane.

It's not that his explanations don't add up, it's the fact that he gives no explanation. Not even a feeble excuse. It's as though I'm an afterthought.

I can only assume that asking about Rose put the final nail in the coffin. Whoever she is, he isn't prepared to enter into dialogue about her, and I allowed myself to believe what little he did say. This time, for me, the only things running through my head are ifs and maybes. Maybe I let him off the hook too easily. Maybe I should have pushed him more. Maybe I should have demanded an answer to my question.

In all truthfulness, I can't blame Mark. I wanted to believe him. As I lay there beneath him, I wanted what he was ready to give. I wanted him so desperately that I accepted what he told me when he promised I didn't have to worry. And for some reason, I still believe him. What I chose to ignore is the fact that he wants casual. So I have no one to blame but myself for the disappointment I feel.

Recognising I'm wondering off into la-la land, Rachel clears her throat to bring me back to the subject at hand. "Because, dummy, he has his own law firm, and lawyers cost money. So I was thinking perhaps he'd give you some free advice."

"Rach, I can't. What will he think?"

"Just call him. What harm can it do?"

I contemplate this for a few seconds and have to admit that I can see the logic in her thinking. "Okay, I guess you're right, it makes sense. I'll call him when I get back to my desk."

***

Having taken Rachel's advice and called Mark, I didn't want to go into too much detail over the phone, so he gave me an appointment the same day, but late enough that I don't have to leave work too early. Which is why, at five forty-five, I'm walking into his plush office on the second floor of an impressive Georgian building in schmancy, fancy Mayfair.

His office is contemporary with built-in bookshelves along the entire length of the wall to my left, stacked with what seems to be every edition of Halsbury's law books. There's a piece of modern art on the wall to my right, which adds splashes of colour to the white walls.

His sleek, uncluttered, modern, rectangular dark-wood desk sits in front of the floor-to-ceiling window, his laptop and a file of papers open.

He stands up and walks around his desk to greet me with a kiss on the cheek, and a genuine, warm smile that spreads across his entire face.

"Hey, how are you?" he asks.

"I'm… good."

"Have a seat." He gestures with his hand to one of the two chairs facing his desk.

He's clearly observant because before he sits opposite me in his own chair, he adjusts the blinds slightly to stop the glare of sunlight shinning directly into my eyes; then he sinks into the comfort of the plush black leather with his back to the window.

He looks almost presidential sitting at his desk in his bespoke suit. Looking every inch the confident, successful man that he is.

"It's good to see you. But you do know that if you want to see me, you don't need to make an appointment." There's a quirk of an eyebrow, and his look is one of quiet amusement.

"It's not a social call that's why I thought it would be best to come to your office. Keep things separate from…" I trail off not wanting to say us, since there is no us.

He doesn't say anything he just continues to stare at me, his expression changing to one of curiosity.

Nervousness has my skin prickling as I remove the envelope from my bag and place my bag on the floor. "I wanted to ask your professional advice about something." How I'm able to keep my voice steady I'll never know.

"So it's legal advice you need? You're not here because you missed me and can't wait to get your hands on me?"

I don't even manage to muster a smile. I simply place the envelope on his desk and slide it towards him.

Recognising I'm not in a joking mood, he instantly demonstrates his professionalism with his ability to remain composed as he takes the envelope and removes its contents. He doesn't show any reaction except to look up and cast a glance at me, then focus back on the document. I, on the other hand, find myself fidgeting. I have my hands in my lap. I inspect my fingernails. I rub my hands along my thighs. Then I cross my arms. I'm so nervous, not about what his advice may be, but about what he will think of me. I'm worried that his opinion of me will change.

He finally places the document on his desk and looks

up. "You've been named as the co-respondent in a divorce petition."

"Yes, I've managed to figure that much out myself."

When he raises his brows in what I can only assume is disapproval, I immediately chastise myself. I've come to him for help. I need to rein in the attitude, no matter how anxious I am. "I'm sorry. I'm just worried about what all this means. What I want to know is, if there's anything I can I do about it, and if so, what?"

He sits back. His fingers steepled under his chin as he sits thoughtfully for a moment. Is he distancing himself from me? Is he repulsed by me?

"Is it true. You had an affair with a married man?"

I bend my head and study my hands. My lids come down over my eyes as I take a deep breath and exhale, then lift my head to look at him. His dark eyes stare back at me expectantly as he awaits my reply. Then I remember that I've nothing to be ashamed of. This I all on Andrew. I did nothing wrong, technically. I hold my head up with dignity as I answer his question.

"Yes, but in my defence, I didn't know he was married. I only found out when his wife turned up on my doorstep. And trust me, I may have been naive, but I wasn't naive enough to believe his promises that he would leave her. I ended it the moment I found out." Even as I say the words, I can't help recognising the contradiction. I don't know what it is or why I find it so hard to stop coming back for more where Mark is concerned.

There's a faint glimmer of relief as I notice his facial muscles relax and a hint of a smile appears as the corners of his mouth curve slightly upwards.

"My area of expertise is corporate law, so my knowledge on divorce is basic, but I'll ask someone in our matrimonial department to take a look. From what I know, it's a pointless tactic. It's most likely for revenge or spite."

I sit, nodding as he picks up the office phone. "Natasha, could you come to my office if you're free."

A few minutes later there's a light knock on the door. He stands as an attractive, slim, medium-height woman with shoulder-length brown hair, dressed in a black trouser suit, enters. Her power suit does nothing to lessen her femininity as she stands in her heels with a composed and a self-assured manner.

"Natasha, this is Lauren Roberts." I stand as she steps forward to shake my hand, and I grasp her hand in greeting. I return her smile with one of my own and sit down again.

"Could we get your advice on this please?" He hands her the petition.

She takes a moment, looks it over and smirks as she shakes her head. "Really, really, ill advised," she says, almost as if she's speaking to herself.

"That was my initial reaction. What can we do about it? Lauren doesn't want to be dragged into their mess."

She turns to me. "Since the wife has made you a party to the proceedings, that means you're expected to respond. However, we can go back to them and say were not inclined to, which will mean not only a delay, but more than likely an increase in expenses on their end. These things can drag on for months, sometimes years if the settlement being sought is extensive. Do you know what the financial situation is?"

"I know they're comfortable, but I doubt we're talking millions," I say.

"I'd go with that then. Stall any response and drag it out

to try to get them to remove you as co-respondent."

My face drops when she says the words "drag it out," and I answer quickly, almost pleading with her. "No, please, I don't want to drag it out. I just want it over and done with." I thought I'd put Andrew well and truly behind me, but it seems he's determined to fuck with my life.

Mark takes charge, speaking calmly but firmly. "Could you deal with this for us, Natasha? I know you have a lot on your plate at the moment."

There's a dismissive wave of a hand as Mark walks her towards the door. "Pfft. This is small fry. I can have this wrapped up by the end of next week. Good to meet you, Lauren." She strolls out with such confidence that I really believe she will have this done and dusted in no time.

Once she leaves the office, I broach another important subject. "How much do you think this will cost me?"

He takes slow steps towards me. With his strong, powerful hands, he pulls me up from the chair. His fingers lightly touch my cheek, his gaze reassuring. "Hey, don't look so worried. Natasha will sort it out for you. And don't worry about the cost."

"But—"

"No buts. What's the point of having a boyfriend with his own law firm if you can't get free advice?"

I lower my head, biting my bottom lip, and nodding, surprised by his generosity. Even more surprised that he actually considers himself my boyfriend, not just friends with benefits when he sees fit to call me. "So we're not over?"

He gently places his fingers under my chin and raises my head so that I'm looking at him. "I'll be all over you tonight."

A genuine smile overtakes my face when I look up at him. His eyes are brilliant and intelligent. After being on tenterhooks all morning, his commanding manner has taken this problem, my problem, in his stride. He's managed to allay my worries, making me feel positive about the situation, that there is no doubt in my mind that what he says is true, Natasha will have the matter delt with sooner rather than later.

It makes me wonder if there isn't anything he can't do. He exudes strength and masculinity, so much so that I can almost feel the confidence emanating from his body.

It doesn't impress me. It doesn't surprise me. It fascinates me. It fills me with excitement; it's so powerful that I can feel my heartbeat thumping.

Today I've seen another glimmer of the caring side of him mixed in with the side that likes to take control, make things happen, taking care of those around him. I love the fun side of him. I even love the alpha side, there's something very seductive about it. He's let his guard down a little and allowed me in. He's behaving as through we are a regular couple in a regular relationship. Although there is nothing regular about the sex.

Maybe I've simply misjudged things. It could be that he's genuinely busy with work. I've been so paranoid after Andrew's stunt that I've painted Mark with the same brush, and that's unfair.

So of course I allow myself to be swept up in him, literally, as one arm locks around my waist and the other rests on my back, pulling me against him. I snuggle into him, wrapping my arms around his neck and pressing my lips to his. It's a slow, drugging kiss, which has me savouring every moment as I'm lost in a whirl of pleasure. A delicious flutter flows through me when I feel his hardness pressed against my thigh.

His lips brush my ear, his breath tickling me, his words thrilling. "That's a promise of what's to come tonight."

Mark

Once I reluctantly let Lauren leave I call Natasha back to my office. She knocks on my door and enters. "You want to see me?"

"Have a seat. Now it's just the two of us, I want to know what you think the likelihood is of getting Lauren removed as co-respondent?"

"I've done so many of these over the years, never had a problem yet. Admittedly some drag out, but mostly it's usually that the wife is pissed off and just wants to make everyone suffer the same way she is. It could be her way of getting back at Lauren. But in all honesty, I suspect that this isn't the first time he's played away from home. Which probably makes her even more determined to put him through the wringer, and unfortunately, Lauren is getting caught in the crossfire."

"If the need arises, and it helps speed things up, throw some money at it."

"How much are we talking?"

"Up to twenty thousand."

She raises an eyebrow. "Is Lauren willing to pay that amount?"

"Lauren won't be paying, I will. But this is to stay strictly between us, do you understand?"

Her eyes study me probingly. "Sure no problem. She must be quite something if you're willing to buy her out of this?"

"Don't start psychoanalysing my motives."

She openly grins at me, amused by my reaction. "Oh come on, we've been friends for over ten years, I've never seen you infatuated with a woman."

"I'm not infatuated. I'm—"

"In love?"

My answer is swift, laced with a trace of frustration. "Stop putting words in my mouth. I was going to say I like her. She doesn't deserve this, and if I can help her out of this mess I want to do it. Don't read anything into it other than that."

"So this is you doing a favour for a friend?" She stares at me with eyes full of mockery and amusement. Barely able to stifle her laughter as she presses her lips together.

"Okay, I admire her. I like her a lot. Are you satisfied now?"

"Is she 'The One'?"

I lean forward in my chair, doing my best to remain deceptively composed but failing miserably. "What is this, twenty questions? Go do the job you're being paid for."

She stands. "You're the boss," she says, her laughter taking over as she leaves the room.

"Yeah, and don't you forget it," I call out with as much authority I can muster in order to at least give the appearance of some sort of semblance of being in control. Trying to convince myself that Natasha didn't just hit the nail on the head.

Do I love her? I've known her for all of two seconds. The mere suggestion of it is absurd. The idea of it is so fucking ridiculous. But the fact that I'm asking myself the question has to mean something, surely? Nope. It's just sex. And if I keep saying it, I may even convince myself that it's true. Even if it is the best sex I've ever had. We're talking mind-blowing-out-of-this-world sex. Lust—heat

—passion. She brings it all out of me in a way no other woman ever has. Extracting every essence from every pore, and she gives it back in equal measure, capturing my heart in the process.

But how can I give her my complete self when I have Rose to think about. She has to be my priority. Rose has to be the centre of my focus and attention. Rose has my unconditional love, and I'm not sure if I have enough to go around—if there's enough of me to give.

I felt for her today. Despite trying to put on a façade and act strong and in control, there was a look of anxiousness on her face. She looked so vulnerable that I wanted to sweep her into my arms and protect her. Be her knight in shining armour. Fight her demons, slay her dragons. The seething anger I initially felt has abated, but I still want to hurt this arsehole of an ex-boyfriend for causing her distress, for inflicting pain. But am I any better? I stupidly branded the word *boyfriend* around. I'm playing with her heart. She's going to fall in love with me, and I'm going to break her heart, which makes me a selfish son of a bitch, and that makes me no less of an arsehole than her ex.

I need to control this situation. Rein things in. Whatever I think it is I feel for Lauren, I can't offer a commitment. And as much as it will pain me to do it, I'll have to be the arsehole. I'll do what I have to for her benefit. It will hurt her in the short term, but it will be for the best in the long run. If I can make her hate me, then she'll get over it a lot easier and a lot quicker.

I promised her tonight, but it has to be our last night together.

CHAPTER 10

Mark

I'm going all out to impress. I've made a reservation at the fanciest restaurant in Mayfair. Good food and fine wine, it all helps in the art of seduction. The great sex I'll be providing.

I want to leisurely savour and consume every single delicious moment. And if this is going to be our last time together, I'm going to make damn well sure it's going to be a night neither of us is going to forget.

We've ordered our food, and Lauren sips her prosecco, fluttering her long, thick lashes at me as I swirl the scotch in my glass.

Despite philosophising to myself the necessity to end whatever this thing with Lauren is, I've no idea why, but I want to delve into her life a little more. She's managed to captivate me not only with her beauty but with her personality. Her laughter is contagious. Her sense of humour gives me relentless enjoyment. I admire her caring side. I want to guard her vulnerable side.

I'm curious to know more than just where she works and her vital statistics. I want to know more personal things. Things about her family.

"Do you have any siblings?"

She nods while finishing her mouthful of food, then answers once she's swallowed. "I have an older brother. You."

"A younger sister. She lives in Spain with her husband and my niece." She smiles. "I assume your parents are retired."

"It's just Mum now. My dad passed away when I was fourteen." Her eyes are misty and wistful, making me feel like shit for bringing up such a painful memory.

"I'm sorry. It's tough at any age, but it must have been crushing when you were so young. I lost my dad a couple of years ago. Heart attack while playing golf." I swiftly move on with my next question in an attempt to lighten the mood. "Favourite season?"

"Spring. I love the abundance of blooms unfolding. Of course I love a vase of fresh flowers, but one day I'd like to have a garden of my own where I can grow as many varieties as I like. What about you?"

"I'd say summer, but English summers are always a fucking washout. So summers abroad, preferably on a yacht somewhere. Favourite holiday destination?"

She leans forward, elbows on the table and rests her chin in her hands. She gazes at me with those round hazel eyes, her beautiful face ethereal, her beauty overwhelming. Her voice soft as silk, sweet as honey. "Somewhere hot with a secluded beach so I can sunbathe with nothing between me and the sun rays except my SPF."

Of course now my fucking dick is straining against my trousers. This woman is going to be the death of me. But I'm going to make damn well sure it's a slow and delectable death, so that I can indulge myself and seize every last crumb of what she has to give.

"What's with the twenty questions? Is this an advanced course in getting to know you?" Her smile deepens into laughter. It's so infectious that I can't stop myself from throwing my head back and laughing with her. I don't think a woman has ever made me laugh like this. I actually feel happy, content. Which only makes me realise that I have to stay on track. While I can't forget how she makes me feel, I have to ignore it. Tonight is to be our last night together, and I must not deviate from that plan.

Lauren

As our laughter subsides and we continue to enjoy our meal, my eyes are drawn towards a woman who seems to be making a beeline for our table. She has lustrous strands of long blonde hair falling past her shoulders.

I watch as male heads can't help looking in her direction to appreciate her slender body, her tight-fitting dress clinging to every curve as she sashays through the restaurant, glorifying in the attention she is clearly aware she's getting. Mark seems oblivious, not even lifting his head to look in her direction.

It's not until she's standing at our table and clears her throat that Mark actually stops cutting into his steak and looks up.

He places his knife and fork down, wipes his mouth with his napkin, sits back in his chair, and smirks. "Christina, what can I do for you?"

"I just thought I'd come over and say hello."

"How positively courteous. Not like you at all."

I hide amusement by quickly grabbing my napkin and covering my mouth. She ignores his comment.

"I was going to call you. After our little get together on

Tuesday, I thought we could do it again."

I'm not sure if I manage to hide my surprise as my body stiffens. This revelation causes bitter jealousy to stir inside me. He cancelled our Tuesday date so he could be with her! I guess he didn't expect to be caught out in a lie. But then he never gave an explanation, so technically, he didn't lie. Bloody semantics.

When my eyes leave her to focus on Mark, I stare blankly at him, my complete disappointment rendering me unable to even muster any display of the sadness I feel.

His eyes stare back at me, assessing me, a small curve of his mouth indicates his amusement. Then I see the change on his face as a shadow of annoyance creeps across his features when he realises I'm not smiling, and I don't find this amusing.

His eyes dart up to Christina giving her a brutal stare —the tone of his voice chilly. "Firstly, I wouldn't categorise your visit to my offices on Tuesday as a get together. You needed legal advice, and for some reason, out of the hundreds of firms available in London, you chose mine. Graham provided that advice, and you will be billed accordingly."

I watch as she stands motionless. Only her face belies her feelings as her brows are pulled into an affronted frown, her mouth is tight and grim as she stares at him glumly.

"Secondly, I'd appreciate it if you would accept the fact that our one night together was just that. One night. Never—To—Be—Repeated. Now, unless it's escaped your notice, I'm on a date, which you've rudely interrupted, and I'd like to get back to it."

He looks away from her dismissively, picks up his knife

and fork, and continues to eat his food.

She retreats without another word, but not before giving me a death stare, as if this is all my fault.

"Well isn't she a bundle of laughs."

"Yeah, amazing how good make-up, expensive clothes, and jewellery can hide a multitude of sins. Trust me, she's no better than a first-class hussy."

I almost choke on my food. "Oh my God, you didn't just say that."

"I call it how it is."

I remain silent. Faced with the realisation that this is how he may describe me one day.
I feel as though I've just had a reality check. "Is that how you see me?"

"Are you fucking with me right now? You, Lauren Roberts, are nothing like her, or any other woman I've ever been with. You have a sense of humour for a start. That's always attractive in a woman. You excite me. You're so fucking sexy I can hardly stay in control of my faculties right now. So for fuck's sake can you hurry up and finish your food so I can get you home and have my dessert."

CHAPTER 11
Lauren

After everything he's done for me with the predicament I found myself in with Andrew, and being dragged into his divorce proceedings, I stupidly read too much into it. The way he took complete control of the situation made me truly believe with a strong resolve that I mean something to him.

Even the way he made love to me the other night felt different. I don't know if it's because of our run in with Christina, and he felt he had to prove something to me, but he seemed to be taking his time, as if to savour me. Each touch of his lips on mine was warm and sweet, tantalizing my senses and desires, making me want him even more than I already do.

There seemed to be a contentment flowing between us. Happiness filled me as he gathered me into his arms and held me so tight, as if he didn't ever want to let go. My curves moulding to the hard contours of his muscular body. Each and every word whispered into my ear sent a shiver through me. Each time our eyes locked there seemed to be an unspoken feeling of endearment. In my wildest dreams I never imagined it could be like this.

But now I'm left feeling confused, because as he was leaving my apartment the other night, he said he would come by my work the next day and take me to lunch. He didn't show up, so I called him. He actually apologised, and we rescheduled, but he cancelled and hasn't called me for four days. I toy with calling him again. I even dial the number but fail to press the call button every single time. Perhaps I should send a text. I dig deep to find something refined to say, something intellectual. Something that would let him know in no uncertain terms exactly what I think. In the end I throw maturity out the window and settle on arsehole.

His constant indecisiveness about us has become tiresome, and he's been able to get away with his behaviour because I've let him. But if I look at things objectively, he's not indecisive. He knows exactly what he wants—sex. He's very sure about that and has made it very clear that's what he wants from me. More fool me for giving him what he wants. But that's because I'm stupid enough to believe he'll fall in love with me the more time we spend together. I've come to the conclusion that I've learned nothing in my twenty-eight years on this planet.

I've lectured myself. I've been telling myself that I shouldn't put up with this constant back and forth. His constant blowing hot and cold behaviour. Going days without contacting me, then only calling me because he wants to get laid. How long does he think I'm going to be at his beck and call? Other women may put up with it; I have to admit the sex is almost worth it, but I'm not sure if I'm capable of being emotionally detached—it's too late for that—I'm already tethered by the invisible, delicate thread that's formed between us. A connection he wants to pretend is not there.

I'm doing everything I can to fight the agonizing and torturous realisation that he cares, but not enough for him to give himself completely to me.

I try my best to make sense of it all. I assess his reasons for helping me with my legal woes, and all I can come up with is that he had a way and a means to assist me, so he did. It's as simple as that, and I shouldn't put any other meaning into it. In fact, I need to put all thoughts of Mark Taylor out of my mind. I can and will put all thoughts of Mark Taylor out of my mind. I need to accept that a happy ever after with Mark is so out of my reach, that no amount of wanting it will make it happen.

I put all my energy into trying to stay focused at work. I do my best to concentrate on campaign strategies. Keeping myself busy works for the most part, but today's date is not lost on me.

Every female in the office is filled with excitement, and some of the guys too, at having received colourful bouquets of roses. The entire office is engulfed by the pungent floral scent as it floats through the air.

While women are gushing around me like lovesick teenagers, I carry on working. I can't recall the last time a guy bought me flowers.

"Hey, Lauren."

I look up to see Rachel walking towards me with a huge bouquet of multicoloured roses. The smile splayed across her face makes it impossible not to be happy for my best friend.

"Wow! They're impressive. Tom has really gone to town this year."

"Oh no. These aren't from Tom."

I waggle my eyebrows at her. "Are you saying you have a secret admirer?"

"Nope. They're for you. Happy Valentine's Day."

I stare at her disbelievingly, then admire the bouquet. "Yeah, right. Who on earth would send me flowers?"

"A certain sexy lawyer perhaps?"

I laugh at the preposterous notion. "Trust me on this one; Mark isn't one for flowers and chocolates. It's out of his comfort zone."

Undeterred she ignores me and continues. "There's a card." She hands it to me and places the bouquet of roses on my desk.

There must be a complete look of confusion on my face as I read the card, which prompts her next question.

"What does it say?"

I hold up the card for her, and she reads aloud. "'I guess I am a flowers and chocolates kind of guy after all.' What does that even mean?"

"I think it's his way of apologising. He's cancelled on me again and hasn't called me since. And I made my thoughts and displeasure known."

My attention is drawn away from Rachel as I spot a delivery guy walking towards us with another bouquet.

"Lauren Roberts?"

"Yes," I say a little apprehensively.

He proceeds to plonk the bouquet of only red roses down on my desk and walks off.

Rachel beams a smile at me. "Wow, I'd say someone's really going to town on asking for forgiveness. Read the card, read the card."

I detach the card from the cellophane wrapping. "It says 'Dinner. Tonight. I'll pick you up at six thirty.'" I let out a frustrated breath. I'm hesitant. Should I give in and meet him?

"You are going, aren't you?" Rachel asks, astute as ever.

"I don't know what to do. It's kind of demanding, don't you think? And pretty arrogant to just assume I'll drop everything and go. In any case, what will it achieve? I don't want to get my hopes up only to have them dashed again. I'm not sure I could take it."

Her voice is soft and caring. "Come on, he's made the first move at an apology. Give him a chance. I have a really good feeling. He's the one, I know it." I roll my eyes at her. "Don't give me that look. You know I'm always right about these things. I have a sixth sense."

"If that's the case how come you couldn't smell the crap Andrew was dishing out."

Her mouth is tight and grim. "He had us all fooled."

Mark

Natasha knocks on my door and enters without waiting for the obligatory permission.

"Take a seat. What can I do for you?"

"I came to give you an update on the Roberts case."

That gets my immediate attention. I stop what I'm doing and put the papers that I'm reading down on my desk. I sit back and gesture with a nod for her to continue.

"Would you like to know how much?"

"I don't know. Would I?"

"Let's just say the soon-to-be ex-wife is cheap, in every sense of the word. Her lawyer practically bit my hand off before I even finished my sentence and was able to name a price. I'll need you to transfer the funds from your personal account to the office account."

"Of course. I'll have it done by the end of the day. But make sure you have the contract signed and in your possession before any money goes to her lawyer."

She nods. "So now that's been taken care of, want to get anything out in the open?"

"Such as?" I know exactly what she means.

"Lauren Roberts. Why are you going the extra mile for her?"

"Why do you think?"

"Well, the last time I was in this office discussing Lauren Roberts with you, you nearly bit my head off. I'm reluctant to suggest the L word again in case I'm sent to the guillotine."

I chuckle in spite of myself. "Funny, very funny."

Her teasing becomes serious as she studies me intently. Humorous banter replaced by intrigue. "So, are you in love with her?"

Yes, I admit it. I'm in love with her. "I think you need to direct your energy at finding yourself a man to occupy you so that you don't have time to interfere in everyone else's love life."

"Ha, I'm only taking an interest in yours since this occurrence is something of an anomaly." She stands up and starts to walk to the door but turns just as she's reaching for the handle. "Oh, and don't think I didn't notice the lack of denial to my question."

She exits with a chuckle before I can even take a breath to reply. I swivel in my chair to look out at the skyline. Thinking of Lauren brings a smile to my face. It's then that I realise I always get the biggest turn-on just at the mere thought of her, without even having sex. There's something about her I can't quite put into words, but when she's around, there's a constant light shining. Everything seems brighter. I'm happier.

The days and nights that I spend with Rose at my apartment are precious, and I won't give them up for anything or anyone. But I can still spend time with Lauren. The two don't have to be mutually inclusive. Maybe I've been overthinking things. Perhaps there's no need for me to guard my feelings and actions. A couple of nights a week should be acceptable to a woman without there being any expectations.

I haven't called her for four days, and she's made her displeasure very clear with her text. I can't say I blame her. In fact I'd go so far as to say I agree with her; I am an arsehole. But this arsehole is determined to try and rectify things.

So with that intention in mind, I decide to do something I've never done when I'm seeing a woman for fear of her attributing any meaning to it. I pick up the phone an order an abundance of flowers to be delivered to her workplace, and for some inexplicable reason, I feel pleased with myself. I actually feel a little romantic. Who the fuck would have thought it possible?

CHAPTER 12

Lauren

I'm just slipping into a red slinky dress when my buzzer goes. He's early.

Of course I accepted his invitation. It felt almost like an impassioned plea. And even though Rachel went through a whole catalogue of reasons why I should accept, I didn't need her to convince me. If I'm truly honest with myself, I know I should be resisting the temptation, but the way I feel about Mark in such a short space of time is totally different to how I've ever felt about anyone. There remains this magnetic pull. It's too intense to ignore.

I scurry excitedly to the intercom and press the entry button. I open the door leaving it ajar and dash back to the bedroom to fetch my shoes.

I hobble along to the living room as I slip my shoes on. "You're just in time to zip me up," I say before looking up.

"Well, well, well. Don't we look ravishing this evening." His words are complimentary, but his tone is hardened, heavy with sarcasm. "Going anywhere special?"

As I put my foot back on the ground I stumble from the shock. I lift my chin to meet his icy stare straight on.

"What the hell are you doing here?"

Andrew pushes the door, but it doesn't quite close. He ambles towards me so that he's right up in my face. My nostrils flare as the air around me is sullied with his odour.

"That's no way to greet an old friend. Why would you assume I want something? Maybe I've missed you and just came to see how you are. Would that be so hard to believe?"

"Yes, it would. When have you ever done anything genuine?"

There's a quick shrug as he glances around, taking in his surroundings. "The place hasn't changed much."

"What are you doing here, Andrew?"

He focuses back on me. "Okay, you're right. I do want something." He looks menacing as his eyes are raking over my body suggestively, causing a nauseating feeling in the pit of my stomach. I swallow the lump in my throat and do my best to keep control, so I don't show any signs of panic or fear. Should I feel panicked or fearful?

He takes one more step, bringing him even closer, allowing him to reach out without warning. His fingers trace a path along my jaw line and down to my shoulder, twisting the spaghetti strap of my dress between his fingers.

I shrug his hand away and attempt to step back, but he grabs my arm possessively, digging his fingers into my flesh, his demeanour becoming determined as he looks at me with a twisted, cold smirk, full of contempt. He seems to be enjoying my struggle to remain composed.

"You know, I can still do it for you, you just need to say the word. I won't even make you beg. You certainly still do it for me, dressed in this sexy little red number. The fact that I know what's beneath is making me hard just thinking about it. Want to feel it?"

The suggestive tone in his voice chills me and his words fill me with dread at the thought of what he's capable of or what he might do.

He presses his body against mine so that I can feel his hard length on my thigh and my body tenses immediately. It makes me nauseous. I actually have the urge to vomit all over his designer suit.

He presses his mouth to my ear. I close my eyes in the hope of visualising something calming, like ocean waves crashing on the shoreline, as his hot breath makes me want to cower in disgust.

His hand moves down to my butt, caressing and squeezing one cheek. "What are you wearing underneath? Red or black? Silk or lace? A thong or those thin little panties that you used to enjoy begging me to tear from your body? I remember how impatient you were. You couldn't wait to spread your legs for me, begging me to fuck you harder. You were my perfect little sex slut. The woman I'm seeing now doesn't quite compare, unfortunately. The sex is all very vanilla. She's nothing like you, she just lays there. Do you know, she was quite shocked when I told her I was going to fuck her so hard she wouldn't be able to walk for a week. That's one of the things I like about you. You love the dirty talk."

I hold in my emotions as best I can. "What are you doing here? What exactly do you want from me?"

It's as though my words have released him from some crazed trance. He loosens his grip, and I take the opportunity to break free from him, stepping back as I hug my arms to myself.

"I want what that boyfriend of yours gave that soon-to-be bitch of an ex-wife of mine. But I want more. Ten thousand pounds is small change. I want more, and I know that he's good for it. I've checked him out."

I can't even fathom what he's talking about. Full of shit as usual. "What are you blabbering on about?"

He surveys me for a moment. There's a look of faint amusement as his eyes rake over me, and his lips twist into a cynical smile.

"You really don't know? Seems that men can't help keeping secrets from you. Must be something in your DNA that has you lacking judgement, or do you enjoy being made a fool of? Is it some sort of helpless damsel in distress fetish? It certainly worked on me. I couldn't get enough of you."

Despite my mind being a whirl of confused thoughts, it's my complete antagonism towards him that gives me a sudden sense of strength and determination, wanting to get to the bottom of this. Wanting to know what he means. So when I speak it's bordering on a snarl.

"For crying out loud, you pathetic specimen for a man. I know you're dying to tell me so just get on with it."

There's a viciousness to his voice. "The divorce. Elizabeth has finally signed the papers. Seems your hot-shot-lawyer boyfriend greased the wheels to speed things along and paid her ten thousand pounds to have you removed as co-respondent."

I laugh in his face. It's an instant reaction to what he's just said. It just seems too ludicrous for words. "Don't be ridiculous. Why would Mark do such a thing?"

"Oh, I don't know, you tell me? There's only one reason I can think of, and that involves you flat on your back. Or do you spend your time bent over with your arse in the air, like you did for me? And here I am thinking I was special. I have to admit, I always had a fondness for that particular position. Pounding into you from behind, dominating you, being able to see myself penetrating you. Remember how you liked it when I grabbed your arse and pulled your hair. You begged for me to impale you with my cock. Do you beg him to fuck you harder like you begged me? Just say the word, and we can revisit those times. I'm getting a bit fed up with vanilla, especially when I've tasted your flavours and the variety you offer."

He comes towards me again, reaches out his hand and slides it down my arm. "Your hot-shot-lawyer friend may be the man of the moment, but I'll always take great pleasure from the fact that I had you before him. I tasted you before him. I was inside you before him. And whatever you do for him, you did for me first."

I can't help myself. I'm so incensed that despite shaking like a leaf, before I know it, before I can stop myself, my palm is making contact with his cheek. Surprise mars his face, but he's not perturbed as he rubs the soreness of his cheek with his hand and laughs in my face.

I start shouting at him, the deep hatred in my own voice coming through loud and clear. "He's nothing like you. I actually enjoy having sex with him. Sex with you was a monotonous chore. I've lost count of the number of times I had to fake it. 'Ooh, Ahh. Yeah baby, right there, just like that. Don't stop.' It wasn't hard, just like you. And unlike you, he actually makes me come, multiple times in one night. You couldn't even keep it up long enough. He's nothing like you. I don't know what I ever saw in you."

"Don't flatter yourself by thinking you're special. Women like you are ten a penny to someone like him. Available at any bar for the price of a drink."

Tears threaten to blind my eyes and choke my voice,

but I'm determined not to let him get the better of me and have the last word.

"You bastard. I don't know what I was thinking when I dated you. Just being here in the same room as you makes me want to throw up." *And to think I once thought I had a future with this piece of shit.* Sometimes not getting what you want can be considered a stroke of luck.

The scowl displayed on his face grows hard as he shoots me a venomous look. His jaw is clenched tight, his nostrils flare, as instinct has him grabbing me with such force he has me whirling around so that I'm locked in his tight clutches with my back to his front.

"I never had you down as a bitch. But looking back, all the evidence was there."

"Let go of me or—"

He growls in my ear. "Or what? I don't think you're in any position to make demands. I could do whatever I want to you right now. Take whatever I want. I have a feeling you may even enjoy it. We never did try the rough stuff. I'm game if you are."

I muster as much strength as I can, raise my foot and kick him in the shin, forcing him to let go of me and recoil in pain.

"You fucking bitch."

"I hate you with every fibre of my body. I love him with every ounce of my being." I hear my words buzz through the room, bouncing off the walls, as I bite down hard on my lower lip. I've tried for so long to deny my feelings for Mark that I've shocked not just Andrew with my admission, but myself. Surprisingly, there's a sense of satisfaction, a feeling of clarity at hearing myself say the words out loud.

But I don't have time to dwell on my thoughts and feelings as I'm hurtled back to reality by the sound of Mark's hardened voice, its sternness laced with a thread of warning.

"What the hell is going on here?"

I feel myself trembling as I turn towards the door to see Mark standing at the threshold. I'm wondering what this must look like to him, what he must be thinking. He casts me a fleeting glance before his tall figure heads towards Andrew, who only moments ago took such delight in trying to instil fear into me with his threats, but now stands motionless and silent.

Mark stands inches from him. Even though they're almost the same in height, Mark is towering over Andrew, who now seems to be recoiling. How quickly the mighty fall.

I look on, almost in wonderment, at how Mark carries himself. Even now, with such anger boiling over, he still manages to maintain the commanding air of self-assurance and control. He still looks devilishly handsome, despite the displeasure evident from his tensed jaw. There's a strength in his face. His compelling eyes are narrowed in anger, his features firm.

"I'll ask again, shall I? What the fuck is happening here?"

Andrew shifts from one foot to the other, unable to keep eye contact with Mark. I notice his hands adjust the cuffs of his suit jacket nervously. He draws a sharp breath before he speaks.

"I was just explaining to Lauren that I think I'm entitled to some sort of recompense. I don't see why I should be left out of pocket."

Mark spits out his words with disdain. "You're the weasel of an ex-boyfriend?"

"I want what's due to me."

"You," says Mark, poking a finger in Andrew's chest, "do not get a penny."

"Why not?" Andrew barks. Then he straightens himself. There's a gleam of satisfaction on his face, as if he's just found the location of the lost City of Atlantis. "Maybe I'll decide not to sign, how about that."

"I don't give a fuck what you do. But before you get too cocky, all I care about is having Lauren removed as corespondent, and that has now been achieved, thanks to your soon-to-be ex-wife's greed. I have to say, she's cheap, almost as cheap as you."

"I can report you to the Solicitors Regulatory Body for having inappropriate relations with a client." He seems positively joyous at coming up with that one.

Mark absent-mindedly cracks his knuckles and gives him a look of absolute indifference. He tilts his head to the side, eyeing him amusingly. "Is that the best you can come up with? I strongly suggest that you get your sorry arse out of here before I do something that may land you in hospital and me in jail. I would also recommend that you stay away from Lauren. If you bother her again, she'll call the police, and I'll get a restraining order. Do I make myself clear?"

Andrew knows when he's beaten. He moves to make a speedy retreat. When he gets to the door, he decides he's not leaving without having the last word.

"You're welcome to her. You may think you're getting the fuck of your life, but she's the one fucking you over. Don't say I didn't warn you." And he rushes out of the door, slamming it closed behind him before Mark can get to him.

There are a few seconds of silence as we stare at each

other. I'm trying to make sense of what just happened. Then I wonder what he's thinking. Is he questioning what he's gotten himself into? I'm barely able to control my reaction to what's just occurred, as my body reacts to the stress of the situation, and I start to tremble. I'm conscious of a lone tear trickling down my cheek, and I wipe it away with my fingertips and then cover my face with both hands.

"Oh God, why does this have to happen to me? What did I ever do to deserve this?"

I feel the instant electricity of Mark's reassuring touch as he comes and takes hold of my hands, moving them away from my face. He wraps his arms around me, and I instinctively bury my head into the hollow between his neck and shoulder, making me feel safe. I wrap my arms tightly around his waist, not wanting to let go, afraid of what may happen if I do.

Then I have an alarming thought. How much did he hear? I lean back and look up at him. "He said some awful things. Truly horrid and hurtful. They're not true. You mustn't believe him."

"Hey, it's okay," he says as he gently strokes the length of my hair with one hand; it seems to have a soothing effect, and I can feel a peacefulness take over as the tension slowly eases out of my body and I begin to relax. He has that natural skill of making me feel safe.

"I'm really sorry. Now our evening is ruined."

"It's not your fault, and nothing is ruined. We can stay home if you prefer not to go out."

"You don't mind? I don't think I can face going out now."

He sweeps me up into his arms and walks to the sofa where he sits down with me in his lap. "Of course I don't mind. We're spending time together. That's all that matters, not where we are."

I tilt my head back to get a good look at him. "Is it true? Did you really pay her off?"

His fingers trace a path up and down my bare arm. "Yes."

There's a jumble of confused thoughts and questions racing through my mind. "Why would you do that? I don't have that sort of money. I can't pay you back. Maybe in instalments?"

"I don't want the money back."

"Then why?"

As he looks at me, a questioning gaze passes between us. "Because I care about you. Is that so hard to believe?"

"Maybe a little. I'm just surprised that's all. Apart from my parents and my brother, I've never really had anyone look out for me. I'm not sure how to respond to such generosity. Or what you expect in return."

"I don't expect anything." His eyes are filled with longing, and I can feel the tenderness in his gaze. I can feel my heart leaping with excitement, and before I know it, without any objection from me, he's carrying me to the bedroom.

While shedding our clothes is rushed, everything else is done sweet and slow. He even puts the condom on ceremoniously, with a captivating smile, as he keeps his eyes glued to mine while he does so. The light of desire that illuminates his eyes makes it all too easy to get lost in this moment.

"I'm going to make it all go away. You're going to forget everything, and when I'm done, you're going to feel so much better."

He slowly moves to cover my body with his, and the

feel of his flesh against mine gives me tingles. His touch is soft and caressing. His mouth peppers soft kisses on my neck and down to my shoulder. And when he sinks into me, he does so slowly and gently, filling me completely.

When he smothers my lips with his, our bodies move together, extracting every inch of pleasure from each other. My body's wants and needs have been awakened, and I let myself go. I allow myself to surrender completely to my desires. I allow myself to accept everything he has to give, and I give back in equal measure until we're skyrocketing to oblivion, gasping in sweet agony.

I get so much pleasure lying close to him, his skin on mine, hot and sweaty. His breath laboured after exertion.

In this moment I know that my words weren't just said to annoy Andrew. I do love Mark. He's in my heart. I can't seem to stop my feelings taking over. They control my every thought, my every willing response. They're like a rapidly spreading fire—uncontrollable.

CHAPTER 13
Lauren

After such an exhausting week at work, when Friday finally comes around, I feel the need to let my hair down, and with that conviction in mind, after work, Rachel and I head out to meet Jules at a new restaurant bar that has opened in Covent Garden, not far from our offices.

Since Jules is pregnant, we're sticking together in solidarity and drinking virgin frozen margaritas. I'm not sure whether it's the atmosphere in the bar or the fact that the three of us are together again, but we seem to be buzzing on excitement. Until that is, Jules brings up the one subject I want to steer clear of. The one person I'm trying to put out of my mind. Because the mere thought of him makes me ache with yearning.

"How are things going with Mark?"

I take a moment to weigh up her question. As my head is in a swirl of confusion trying to navigate through the haze of feelings, I drop my shoulders with a sigh. "I'm confused."

Her brows draw together, confirming her own confusion. "What about?"

"I have an unsettling feeling."

"Explain," says Rachel.

"When we're together, everything is almost perfect."

"Almost?"

They're both fixated on me, waiting for my response. "I just keep getting this nagging feeling in the back of my mind, which refuses to go away. I think there's someone else."

"Don't be ridiculous. I know Mark, he's not like that. Sure, he likes women, but Adam says he's never had two women on the go at the same time. To be honest, I doubt he has time for that even if he wanted to. What makes you even think such a thing?"

"It's lots of different things. Two weeks ago, when Andrew showed up at my apartment being menacing, Mark took complete control of the situation. And when we made love later that night, I really felt as if we're getting closer. He admitted to me that he cares about me. Maybe he's regretting that admission and now it feels like a carefully constructed plan, as if he's purposefully pulling back in order to stop me from getting any ideas about us. Cancelled dates. Secretive phone calls. We spend wonderful nights together, then I don't hear from him for days. What else could it be other than another woman? It's the only logical explanation."

"There's Shelby. I've met her a few times. They've known each other for years— they go way back. They have a history together."

I instantly pounce on her statement. "Why haven't you mentioned her before?"

She shrugs. "I didn't consider it relevant."

I'm biting my lip as the question hammers at me. I need to pull as many pieces as possible together, so I can get the full picture. "What do you know about Rose?"

She seems startled by my question. She hesitates slightly. She thinks she's gotten away with it and that I haven't noticed how she's looking around her, focussing her eyes on anything but me.

She answers with a question of her own. "How do you know about Rose?"

"Don't try and deflect."

"I'm not supposed to talk about Rose with Mark's women."

Her words unleash not only frustration, but disbelief, which makes me almost scream at her. "Oh—My—God. I'm not one of Mark's women. I'm your best friend. I can't believe you know something, and you won't tell me."

Her response is cryptic. "Please don't be angry with me. Mark wants his private life to remain just that, and I have to respect his wishes. It's not my place. He would literally flip if he knew we were even discussing her, and so would Adam for that matter if he knew I'd broken a confidence."

"Seriously, your putting dick before girl code."

"No, I'm putting my husband before girl code. There's a difference."

"Just tell me one thing. Should I be worried about her coming between Mark and me?" I hold my hand up to pre-empt any reply. "Actually, you know what, don't bother answering that. Because it seems she already has. I really can't believe you've kept this to yourself. You of all people."

"What's that supposed to mean?"

"Rachel and I were by your side, ready to pick up the pieces when you were seeing Adam. We had your back. Why is it so hard for you to do the same for me? Rach help me out here."

"I think you both need to calm down. Shouting at each other isn't doing anyone any good. Think about the baby."

I glance at Jules, her worried frown staring back at me, and suddenly I feel full of remorse. "Oh Jesus. I'm sorry." I scoot nearer to her and give her a hug. "I know it's not your fault. It's no one's fault except Mark's. And perhaps mine for purposely ignoring the little things niggling at me."

"I'm sorry too. I wanted to tell you, but Adam told me to let things play out. I was stuck between a rock and a hard place."

"But you're still not going to tell me anything about Rose?"

She shakes her head. "I'm sorry. If he wants you to know, he'll tell you himself."

"I guess we know the answer to that one." I shudder inwardly at the realisation.

There're a few seconds of silence as no one knows what to say. Then it's broken by Rachel with her happy-go-lucky cheerfulness. "Now that's sorted, have you thought about actually talking to Mark?" she asks.

"How am I supposed to talk to him if he doesn't want to have any discussion whatsoever about us as a couple. I've lost count how many times he's avoided the subject. He always manages to shut me up with his swoon-worthy kisses and the persuasiveness of his touch. The fact that I haven't heard from him makes me feel like shit because we had one of the best nights ever. The sex is always out of this world, but this last time felt different. And that he actually admitted he cares about me, surely that's got to be worth something?"

Before either of them answers, I continue. "To be honest, I don't think it really matters anymore. I doubt there's anything I can do. Even though I've fallen for him, I've resigned myself to being given the cold shoulder. What started out as a bit of fun with the groomsman has ended up with me giving my heart. And for what? I just want to be so over him that I can go a whole day without thinking or talking about him. I can't put myself through this anymore. I'm so tired of playing a game of which I don't know the rules. I wish I could turn the clock back to the wedding reception."

Rachel sits on her stool swivelling left to right restlessly. Her mouth twitching, waiting for an invitation to speak.

"Okay, Rach. I can see you have something to say."

She stops swivelling and jumps right in without missing a beat. "What if you could go back? What would you do differently?"

I let out a long, frustrated sigh. "Oh, I don't know. Maybe I wouldn't be so enthralled by him and the attention he gave me. I wouldn't get all giddy inside when he made suggestive comments. I wouldn't have spent the night with the groomsman, in his room having multiple orgasms. I'm stupid. Why am I so stupid? I should have seen this coming."

"It's not stupid. You're not stupid. Lesser women have fallen for his charms," says Jules.

I sit up straight and raise my brow curiously. "How many women?"

"You're missing the point. Why would you be any different?"

"And you've hit the nail on the head. I'm not different, am I? I'm just like all the others falling at his feet, or dick, as the case may be."

"I didn't mean it like that, and you know it. You are

different. Even Adam has said Mark isn't acting like himself."

"He has? What exactly has he said? On second thoughts I don't want to know. It's pure conjecture. We need to stick with what we know. The evidence—facts. I need to take off my rose-tinted glasses. Look at things from his perspective. It's lust, that's what's driving his desire. There's no honeymoon phase because he's not looking at this, at us, as something serious. I'm just the flavour of the moment. Falling in love is not on his agenda. And when the lust wears off, what then? You need more than just a strong sexual desire to have anything meaningful. Clearly he's had his fill already, that's why he hasn't called me."

"Perhaps he's taking it slow," says Jules.

I openly laugh. "Yeah, the slow boat to China." I glance at Rachel as she sips her drink while trying to look uninterested in our conversation. "You're quiet, Rachel, very unlike you. No words of wisdom or encouragement?"

She shakes her head then just says, "Nope."

Jules and I both stare wide-eyed in complete surprise. "No?"

"Wow! Never thought I'd see the day," says Jules.

"I don't think you want to hear what I have to say," says Rachel.

"That's never stopped you before," I say.

"Okay, but if you don't like what you hear, don't shoot the messenger. Agreed?"

Jules and I both nod in agreement.

"I've only met him a handful of times, so my opinion is based on a limited amount of interaction."

"Pray do tell us, we're on the edge of our seats. What is your opinion?"

"He's confused. Nervous even. Which is most likely what's making him hesitant."

"Afraid of what?" It's too ridiculous for words. Mark Taylor doesn't do afraid. Aside from Adam, he's the most confident, assertive man I've ever met.

"His own feelings. He's not prepared. Wasn't expecting it or you."

"Christ almighty, and you've got this from the few times you've met him. What exactly did you talk about?"

"It's not necessarily anything he said. I watched mainly."

"Watched?"

"Observed."

She takes another sip of her drink as she straightens herself on her stool; the corners of her mouth curve into a knowing smile, waiting for the inevitable.

I can't say I'm not somewhat intrigued. "Okay, I give in. Observed what?"

"The way he looks at you. How attentive he is. The way his eyes follow you across the room when you leave his side. The look of jealousy when he notices another man talking to you or looking at you. It was clear as day at the wedding reception."

"Oh please. Stop right there. I think you must have had one too many glasses of champagne. Either way, none of that has anything to do with him having feelings for me. It's to do with him being an alpha male. His attentiveness is just him being a gentleman. Take it from me, he has absolutely no interest other than fucking. It's more likely that he doesn't want anyone sniffing around and encroaching on what he considers his territory while he's taking every morsel of pleasure and delight. The incident with Andrew being a prime example. He found him sniffing around something he hadn't quite finished with and did the equivalent of pissing on me to warn him off. Trust me, Mark Taylor is hardwired to do two things. Fuck and fuck hard."

Rachel shrugs her shoulders. "I said you wouldn't like it."

"I just don't agree with your 'observations' that's all. Now can we please change the subject. I'm trying my best to put Mark Taylor out of my mind and forget all about him."

Jules claps her hands together excitedly. "Ooh, tell me about your campaign for the dildo company."

I waggle my brows at her. "Why the sudden interest in rubber toys?"

"I'm just curious." There's a mischievous grin as she looks at me.

"If I recall correctly from listening to your endless bragging, you are in no need of such assistance, or is Adam not performing well these days?"

"Hey, he's performing very well thank you. How do you think I got into this condition?" She gently rubs her protruding stomach.

"Yes, well, I think I could've given you a run for your money on bragging rights if things progressed with… nope I won't say his name."

I watch their animated expressions as I recount everything I've been doing for the campaign. Their eyes grow wide with amusement as they're unable to contain their laughter any longer. It's so infectious that I can't help laughing along with them.

It's a feeling of reassurance, being able to laugh when you really want to cry. It lets you know that things could always be worse, and for someone, somewhere, they probably are. This blip on my romantic life is not the end of the world.

That thought gives me a feeling of confidence, which I hadn't realised I'd lost. But that feeling doesn't last very long. I thought I was doing pretty well until I see Mark stroll in with an Amazonian beauty on his arm.

The three of us are in a corner, so he doesn't notice us.

My first instinct is to go over and give him a piece of my mind for his treatment of me, but I don't. That would only give him the satisfaction of knowing it bothers me. It would also be rather childish of me.

I pull my eyes away from him and flip open the menu. "Let's order some food."

"You've seen him, then?" asks Jules.

"Yes, who hasn't. Hard to avoid him with that on his arm."

"She's quite stunning. I wonder who she is," says Rachel.

"The next in line, clearly. Perhaps that's Rose. Either way, he doesn't waste any time, I'll give him that."

I attract the attention of the server and once we've given our order, Lauren continues with the topic of conversation. "I'm sorry, Lauren. I know you like him a lot."

I can feel Jules's disappointment as she commiserates with me. My own disappointment weighing heavy in my chest. "Yeah, I seem to have a knack for picking unavailable men. The last one was married, and this one it would seem is a bit of a playboy." I let out a deep sigh. "I'm not sure how much more I can take to be honest. Maybe it's my own fault. Maybe I'm giving out the wrong signals?"

"You've had a run of bad luck, that's all. Anyway, I think you two make a great couple. I still have hopes for you even if you don't. I've been watching them. They're not being touchy-feely. They're smiling, but there's no laughter. She's not flicking her hair or pushing her chest out. It all seems serious. Maybe she's a client? Yes, that's it. Definitely a client," says Rachel.

"Maybe. But that still doesn't explain why I haven't heard from him for two whole weeks. Even if this is just sexual gratification, you'd think he'd be a little more courteous and have the decency to actually dump me instead of texting me to cancel a date and then ghost me, leaving me no option but to conclude that he's moving on. He's a little old for that behaviour, don't you think?"

"Maybe he's been busy. There could be a whole host of reasons why he hasn't called. Why are you assuming he's dumped you? Plus, it's early days in your relationship. Tom would go a whole week without calling me when we first started dating. I think you're making too big a deal of it. And since this is the twenty-first century. Why don't you pick the phone up and call him?"

"Because I don't want to appear desperate. Because I don't want to scare him away. But I guess that's clearly something I no longer need to worry about."

"I think you're overthinking things. If his lack of telecommunications is his only flaw, then I say stick with it. Don't write him off too quickly, especially since you really like him."

"Rach, don't you ever get tired of being so optimistic?"

"Ha-ha. May I remind you that it was Moi, who saw what was between Jules and Adam while the pair of you thought I was crazy, and Jules had all but given up on him."

"Yes, but there's a difference. Adam was in love with Jules. Let's face facts and resign ourselves to the reality of the situation."

"Which is?" asks Jules.

"That my little dalliance with the groomsman is over."

Our food arrives just at the right moment, and we swiftly tuck into the deliciousness that has been placed before us, leaving no room for idle chatter or Mark Taylor related talk.

I don't admit to Rachel and Jules that I'm already in love with him.

CHAPTER 14
Lauren

I'm not a stalker, but after seeing him at the bar on Friday evening with a beautiful woman, I'll readily admit it's made me jealous.

I tried not to stare. I tried to hide the fact that every nerve cell in my body was reacting to him being there. I watched him sip his drink. I noticed as he leaned in to listen. I looked out for tell-tale signs that indicated what they were to each other. I didn't get any conclusive evidence.

But when they left after only an hour, that's when the jealousy really took hold of me, clinging on tightly. I watched as he put his hand on the small of her back as they walked out. This gesture alone caused me to spend the entire weekend wondering if they went to his place or hers. Or was their desire for each other so intense that they were unable to wait and headed for the convenient five-star hotel across the street.

Anyone will tell you—it's a fact—a jealous woman is a desperate woman. And desperate times call for desperate measures. So, today, straight after work, before I talk myself out of it, and running on adrenalin, I'm sitting in the back of a cab heading towards his apartment. It's only once I've passed the concierge, who waves a hello in recognition, and I'm in the lift pushing the button for his floor, that I actually start to wonder what the hell I'm doing. In what shape or form is this going to be beneficial?

When Andrew's wife came knocking on my door to confront me, throwing her accusations at me, I told her in no uncertain terms that he presented himself as a single guy. I was not responsible for the fact he couldn't keep it in his pants. What did she gain from venting her anger at me? My sympathy. My pity. But that's about it.

Granted, Mark and I aren't married in this little scenario, so I don't have any claims on him. So what exactly am I hoping to achieve? What exactly do I expect to find? And what do I intend to do when I find it? There's a quote, I can't recall it exactly, or who said it, something about don't look too hard, you may not like what you find. Too late now.

And in the grand scheme of things, what bloody difference does any of it make now that things are over. Does it simply boil down to curiosity? Or is this going to give me closure? Is that what I'm after?

Before I can answer my own questions, the lift doors slide open.

It's as though I'm in a trance as I take the few steps inching me closer to his door, until I find myself standing there, motionless, wondering what to do now. This all seemed like a good idea at the time.

But now I'm not sure what I'm going to say when he answers. If he answers. Maybe he's not even home; it's still early, he's most likely still at the office. But someone must be home, otherwise the concierge would not have let me up.

Did she stay the whole weekend? Even I never had that privilege bestowed upon me.

With a renewed determination, I ring the buzzer.

Nobody answers on the first ring, so I ring again. It's another minute or so before the door opens.

Another second for my jaw to drop to the floor.

"Can I help you?"

The young woman standing before me in cut-off denim shorts and a Blondie T-shirt can only be all of twenty years old; does she even know who Blondie are?

She's towel drying her black hair. She clearly feels sufficiently at home in Mark's apartment to make use of his shower.

I can't help scrutinizing her. She's about five foot five. Slim. Her legs are shapely and toned, her perky little breasts accentuated by her tight-fitting T-shirt. Her pink, bow-shaped lips manage a small non-committal smile. She's make-up free. Her brown eyes are staring at me curiously. Her long lashes flutter as she blinks. She's absolutely gorgeous.

My words come out in a stutter. "I… I came to see Mark."

"He's not here at the moment. I'm not sure what time he'll be home. I can give him a message if you'd like."

Hmm, so she's going to be here for the evening too. How positively domestic.

She doesn't seem the least bit concerned to have another woman at his door. She hasn't asked who I am or what I want. If the roles were reversed, I'd certainly want to know. Perhaps her lack of concern is because she knows he's serious about her?

With that thought in mind, I accept the situation and

decide to cut my losses—make my retreat. I can't fight for someone who's already given himself to another.

"No, it's fine. I'm sorry to have bothered you." But before I turn to leave, my stubborn curiosity gets the better of me, and I can't help asking one more question. "What did you say your name was?"

"I didn't. But it's Rose."

Shock siphons the blood from my face. *Have you met Rose? Mark wants his private life to remain just that.* Everything goes blank for a few seconds as a wave of surprise surges over me. I fight to control the swirl of emotions running through me, and when I refocus my gaze, she's waving her hand in front of my face.

"Hello. Hello. Are you okay?" Despite her question, her expression is one of complete indifference.

"I'm fine. Thanks. Sorry to disturb you." If it's closure I wanted, I've certainly got it.

She shrugs offhandedly, and as she closes the door on me, I hear the word "Weirdo" muttered.

I fight hard to keep my composure as I walk the streets heading to the bar because only alcohol will numb the pain I'm feeling. The intention is to get drunk—drown my sorrows—try to forget my shitty luck when it comes to men.

From the moment I walk into the bar, there's a welcoming vibe. It's barely seven o'clock, but it's busy so I consider myself lucky to get a seat at the bar.

"Hey, Lauren. What can I get you?"

"Hi, the usual please." I'm doing my best to keep to myself, chugging down my margarita like there's no tomorrow.

I pick my empty glass up and gesture to the barman. "Hey, Jason, same again."

He places the glass in front of me. "I appreciate the compliment, but you know full well my name is Sam."

"Sure I do, but perhaps I prefer for you to be Jason. It propels my imagination. What are you doing after your shift?" I take a sip, watching him over the rim of the glass.

He leans in, arms resting on the bar. "Lauren, whatever is going on with you, this is not the answer."

"You're a bartender. That kind of negates you telling me not to drink, don't you think?"

He walks off and has a word with his colleague, then comes back to me. "I wasn't talking about the drink. Why don't you tell me what's wrong? I'm a good listener. Jake can hold the fort."

I slide my empty glass towards him. "I'll have another please, barman."

He watches me with a critical squint. It's only when I huff and puff my impatience that he replenishes my glass, placing it down in front of me.

He remains there, leaning on the bar, waiting. I roll my eyes before speaking. "I'm seeing this guy. Correction! Was seeing a guy."

"The suit."

"You've noticed?"

"Hard to ignore."

"I went to his apartment this evening, uninvited, and a young woman answered the door. I mean, I'm nine years younger than him. How much younger can he go?"

"What exactly is your problem? Is it that he's seeing another woman or that she's younger?"

"It's both. I suppose I'm jealous. I thought, correction, wanted him all to myself. She couldn't have been much older than twenty for crying out loud. It's creepy." I take a large swig, emptying my glass, and gesture for a refill.

"I think you've had enough."

I respond sharply. "I'll decide that. Why don't you just do your job."

His left brow rises a fraction, clearly not impressed by my irritability. There's always been a gentleness to him, despite the rough and ready look, and the arms covered in tattoos, which only serves to make me feel like the bitch that I am right now. But it's when I see the brilliance of his blue eyes looking back at me with calmness and understanding that I feel shamefaced for taking his concern as interference.

"Oh God. I'm so sorry, Sam. Please forgive me." I throw my hands over my face in embarrassment, but just as quickly I feel Sam's strong hands cover mine and gently pull them away from my face.

True to form, he smiles at me without a hint of animosity, and when he gives me a wink, I know all is forgiven.

Sometimes I wonder why we never tried to make a go of things. The sex was great. We both clearly like each other. Ultimately, I know that although there is a great fondness for each other, it's born out of friendship, not love. He wants to be able hit the road at a moment's notice and getting serious with a woman would hinder that. But I'm blessed and grateful to have his friendship.

As I stare into my empty glass, I'm vaguely aware that the seat next to me is vacated but quickly filled.

"Can I buy you a drink?" a smooth, deep voice asks.

"I'll have the same again," I say without looking up.

"Barman, I'll have a scotch on the rocks and whatever the lady is having."

Sam hovers for a moment, and it's only when I look up at him that I notice he's staring at me, a thin smile on his lips, his eyes sending me a private message, letting me know of his misgivings about this situation.

My companion clears his throat, and Sam sets about making our drinks.

"I'm Dean."

I turn to actually look at him. He's not bad looking. Dark blond hair, blue eyes, neat beard, square jawline. Expensive suite. "I'm Lauren."

"Tell me, Lauren, what's a beautiful woman like you doing drinking on her own?"

"Tough day at work. I just need to relax and unwind a little."

"From where I'm sitting your body looks pretty relaxed, and may I say, very sexy."

It's after my fourth margarita that Dean starts to get touchy feely, putting a hand on my thigh and leaning in close whispering God knows what in my ear. I'm not sure if it's the drink, or the fact that I need some sort of comfort and reassurance that I'm still attractive and desirable, but for a few short seconds, I feel a newly awakened sense of worthiness. But then I start to feel irritated by him, and I stiffen when I look down at his hand on my thigh, repulsed when he gives a little squeeze.

I haven't had so much to drink that I'm unable to see with sudden clarity that I need to stop this in its tracks.

"How about we get out of here? I don't live very far. It seems to me that you're in need of good time. Maybe I can help with that."

But I don't get a chance to politely turn him down.

"Get your fucking hands off her. She's not going anywhere with you."

I whip my head around, causing me to feel dizzy. Although I'd put money on it more than likely being the booze.

"Mark!"

"Who the fuck are you?" says Dean.

Mark's tall figure moves from behind me so that he's standing between Dean and me. He repeats his command with such contempt that I can feel the anger in his stern words, and the sheer adrenalin emanating from his body.

"Take your hands off before I do it for you."

There's a scrape of the bar stool on the wooden floor as Dean hastily jumps to his feet and holds his hands up in a surrendering gesture. "Hey, man, you can't blame a guy for trying. She didn't have any objection."

Mark laughs in his face bitterly. "She's drunk, or is that your modus operandi?"

Sufficiently humiliated, Dean grabs his unfinished drink and storms off without another word.

Mark sits in the vacated stool, resting one arm on the bar. He nods in the direction of my glass. "How much have you had to drink?"

"I'm not counting, and it's none of your business. You have no right to interrupt whatever was going on."

He's eyeing me speculatively. "Are you telling me that you would have gone home with that guy, seriously?"

"Maybe, maybe not. But that was my decision to make, not yours. Perhaps I just enjoyed being the centre of attention for a change. Having a man pay me compliments, making me feel desirable. Wanting to spend time with me." I have a sudden thought as I tilt my head to one side and stare at him. "How did you know I was here?"

His brows crease, and he's eyeing me with what can only be described as bewilderment as he finally answers my question. "Sam called me. He got my number from the restaurant bookings log. Do you want to tell me what's going on?"

I swivel my stool and rest my elbows on the bar so I can take a sip of my drink, but my glass is empty. I give a shrug of resignation as my index finger lightly circles the rim of the glass to collect the remainder of the salt, and I proceed with slow and steady licks, flicking my tongue over the tip to ensure I've lapped up every grain from my finger. I don't fail to notice the bulge in his pants as he shifts on his stool, which gives me a sense of achievement at being able to do that to him. Then I remember that I won't be doing it for him anymore. He has someone new to do it for him, which makes me feel crestfallen.

I lift my head to look at him. Despite his handsome face looking solemn, it still sets my heart aflutter. His eyes are fixed on me, waiting.

"I finally decided to take matters into my own hands. I acquired the clarification I needed this evening about exactly where I stand with you. Not that I should've needed it since you've completely cut off all communication with me. I didn't even get the courtesy of an explanation."

"What's that supposed to mean?" The hint of exasperation in his voice is hard to ignore as his words drift into the air. I think I've finally managed to rattle his cage.

I stop toying with my glass and sit upright. "Look, I know this isn't… wasn't supposed to be anything serious for you, but I liked you. Okay, I really liked you. I suppose I'm disappointed because I thought you liked me too. I stupidly thought we went beyond just the sex. But seeing that young woman at your apartment gave me the reality check I needed. Plus I'm a little grossed out at how young you seem to like your women. Anyway, it's fine. I'm out of the picture, so you can carry on however you please with whomever you wish."

He stands up. "Come on, let's get you home."

"Is that it? That's all you have to say. Well, that was anticlimactic."

"If it's a climax you want, I can help you with that."

"That comment is so typical of you."

Managing to successfully disarm me with his charismatic smile, before I know it, he's helping me out of a cab and up to his apartment. I must be two sheets to the wind if I haven't made any objection to him bringing me here.

Once we're inside I look around me curiously. "Where is she?"

"Who?"

Did I go to the wrong apartment? "Please don't pretend I didn't see what I did."

"We'll talk about it in the morning. For now you need to sleep it off."

"You're not going to sleep with me?" *Why am I so disappointed? That's the last thing I should do.*

"Unlike your friend earlier, I don't take advantage of women, drunk or otherwise."

After undressing me and making sure I'm comfortably ensconced in his bed, he kisses the top of my head. I'm not sure if it's voices in my head, but I swear I hear the words "Please know I care about you," then he turns the light off and leaves the room.

CHAPTER 15

Lauren

I'm wide awake, staring aimlessly at the ceiling when the bedroom door swings open. I direct my eyes to the door and see Mark standing there, holding a tray. But that's not all I notice. He's wearing only his sweatpants, and I rake over his torso, the sight of his six-pack, his muscular arms, his strong shoulders. They're all calling to me, and I have to fight my overwhelming need to be close to him. I blink and rub the sleep from my eyes and look again; yep, still there, not a mirage.

I don't remember everything about yesterday, but I distinctly recall asking him to sleep with me. To his credit he didn't even make a twitch of move on me, he kept his hands firmly to himself, despite the invitation. It sure would be a predatory thing to do in my state. But Mark is not a predator. His actions last night lead me to believe that he cares about me. The fact that he was a gentleman and didn't try anything has me feeling embarrassed at my behaviour. But I'm also wondering what the heck is going on. Why did he bring me here instead of taking me home? Am I reading too much into everything?

Maybe this isn't over. Does he want to go back to sleeping together without committing? Are we friends with benefits or are we more than that? I wonder what it is he truly wants from me.

The other remaining question is, if he doesn't care, why does he keep coming to my rescue? Why show up at the bar? More importantly, why does he inch closer only to then pull away?

With these endless inward questions running through my mind, I sit upright and prop my pillow against the headboard.

"Good morning," he says. His greeting is warm and enchanting, and I detect a hint of humour as he moves towards the bed and places the tray down in the middle, then lowers himself onto the bed next to me, making himself comfortable as he sits back, folding his arms across his body.

There's a bemused smile on my lips as I draw my brows together. I'm really not sure what to make of any of this. All my conflicting emotions are welded together in an upsurge of confusion. I don't know where I am with him. One minute he's doing he's damnedest to keep me at arm's length, the next he's turning up at bars and rescuing me from myself. His actions are so confusing. My emotions are tormented by the back and forth. I don't know what to believe or what to make of it anymore. Maybe I'm overanalysing things. But that's because I've fallen hard for him. So hard in fact that it seems my heart is refusing to accept what my mind tells me; it's closing the door, and despite some of yesterday remaining more than a little hazy, it's ignoring the events at the bar that have led to me ending up here in the first place.

His smooth voice interrupts my thoughts. "Don't look so worried. It's just breakfast. I can't send you off into the world without giving you the most important meal of the day."

I glance at the tray in appreciation. He's prepared scrambled eggs, toast, and orange juice.

"What about you?"

"I've eaten already. I'm more of a cereal kind of guy."

"Really, what cereal is your favourite?" I pick up a piece of toast and take a bite as I await his reply.

He clears his throat and mumbles something, but I'm not really sure I hear correctly. There's a slight snicker in my voice as I do my best not to laugh.

"Did you say Cheerios?"

He suddenly sits up proud and with purpose, chest puffed out. "Actually, Honey Nut Cheerios, if you must know."

"Huh, I figured you for a muesli guy." I take a sip of my juice to avoid laughing.

As I continue to consume my breakfast, he watches me as I gobble down every morsel of food and gulp every drop of orange juice.

He shakes his head with a chuckle, whilst inspecting the tray. "Well, someone has a hearty appetite this morning."

"I guess it's the margaritas I had yesterday." When I'm done, he takes the tray and places it on the floor, and I beam a smile of thanks.

I know instinctively what's on his mind as he climbs back on the bed, and his tall frame moves up so that he's straddling me. "Now that you've had your fuel, are you feeling energetic?"

The logical part of my brain tells me I shouldn't go there, that it will be telling him I accept the casual circumstances of our relationship. I don't want a friends-with-benefits arrangement. But then the other part of my brain, the foolish part, tells me I should be selfish. I should just take what's on offer.

He looks at me with his dreamy eyes, their excitement adding to their allure.

I shake my head at him. "Stop looking at me like that."

"How am I looking at you?"

I give him a slow, secret smile. "Like you want to do naughty things to me."

His fingers lightly stroke my cheek. "Can you blame me? You're in my bed, practically naked."

"Is that why you brought me here, to have sex?"

"No, but why not take the opportunity now it's presented itself." It's become very apparent that I've no control when it comes to Mark. If I want anything to come of this, then I need to believe him. Trust him when he tells me I've no need to worry about anything. How can I resist him? I'm only human.

I waggle my brows and give a suggestive smile. "I suppose it all depends on what you have in mind."

I remain motionless for a moment, licking my lips in anticipation, as he stands, drops his sweatpants, grabs a condom from the nightstand drawer and rolls it on, then gently eases himself onto the bed and over my body.

His hands run along my thighs, up my arms and cup my breasts as his demanding lips instinctively find mine and caress my mouth. His tongue explores and probes. His kisses are always rewarding. He pulls gently at my legs so that I'm eased into lying down. It's as though he can read my mind, knowing that all I want right now is for him to make love to me. It thrills me to know that he wants me, that he wants to make love to me. Is he making love to me or is he fucking me? Either way, I can't escape the pleasure our intimacy gives me. I can't supress my attraction to him. My defences are already weakened by the pounding in my heart and quickened pulse at every touch. There's a hot ache in my core at every thrust as I rise to meet him with uncontrolled passion. Ecstasy inching through my veins.

"God, Lauren, you're so beautiful. I want you so much."

Mark

I swore to myself I wouldn't do this to her. I told myself I'd keep having sex with her so long as it remained non-committal and she was happy to continue with that arrangement. I philosophised that we would keep at it so long as we were both being fulfilled. I promised myself I'd only do whatever she would let me do to her for however long we could keep this casual. And even though the guilt will eventually eat at me, it seems I can't control what's coiled in my body, begging for the release that only she can give me. When I'm with her, I'm oblivious to the world around us. Nothing else exists.

I get lost in her, lost in my thoughts, daydreaming about making her mine forever.

And I have no right to have such thoughts.

Maybe I shouldn't be surprised by this unpredictable woman. It's not just her physical attributes, although her curves drive me insane. It's the way her hazel eyes cast a seductive glance at me. It's her rosy lips tempting and tantalising, making me want to take as many kisses from her as I can and savour every single one.

Now I'm more certain than ever that I'm being an utterly selfish bastard, and she has no idea. But as I plunge my length into her tightness I forget all thoughts of staying in control. Because she drives me crazy. I've been unable to stop thinking about her. I need her so badly. And it's only now that I'm realizing that I completely underestimated how powerful her allure is.

There's a gasp as I lower my body over hers. "Let me hear you say my name. I want to hear your sexy little moans."

Her eyes are closed, and she's biting her bottom lip as she lets out breathy moans beneath me. I can't decide which part of her to devour next. I thrust harder and deeper as she moves beneath me, her hips grinding against mine, letting me know how much she wants this, how much she enjoys this.

"Look at me," I say in a whisper. Her eyes flutter open. "You like that, baby?"

She nods.

"Do you want it harder?"

Another nod. "Don't stop. You feel so good."

I fuck her like a man possessed. Driving my hard cock into her warmth as one hand fondles her breasts, then just a light touch with my fingers, teasing her nipples. She moans softly when my tongue explores the rosy buds. She tastes so good.

"God, you drive me fucking insane. Spread those legs and take me in, all of me." My voice is gruff, and it comes out almost as a demand, but she doesn't hesitate to spread herself for me, her wetness providing the lubrication my cock needs to slide smoothly in and out of her folds. Being inside her feels fucking unbelievable. I'm surrounded by warmth.

The glow of pleasure in her eyes is momentarily replaced by a flash of humour. "You say the sweetest things." I silence her with my mouth. Smothering her lips with demanding mastery. Devouring her like a last meal.

Our bodies are in complete sync as we climb to our high together. She squeezes me like a vice, and I let out a roar as I explode inside her. The sound of her exquisite cries of pleasure, and knowing I did that for her, add to my own euphoria.

I collapse breathless beside her. She's panting from the sheer high she's coming down from. I turn on my side to face her. I prop myself up on my elbow and gently push a strand of hair from her face. "You're so sexy, you know that?"

She turns and smiles at me, a mischievous smile. After a few minutes, she sits up and pushes me back. And what she says and does next just about does me in.

"Lie back—relax—enjoy. I want to taste you." She runs her hands over my body and down my thighs as she positions herself.

Her tongue is licking and swirling. Her perfect little mouth takes me in and starts off slow. Sucking and licking my head as her hands are stroking. When she increases the pressure, I wrap my fingers in her hair gently tugging as her head bobs up and down. But it's when she starts to moan, with my cock hitting the back of her throat, that I can't hold back any longer, and I pull her off and up into my arms just as I erupt.

"Jesus, you're killing me woman."

She briefly closes her eyes as her tongue darts out and sweeps across her bottom lip, savouring my taste, then she crashes her mouth to mine so I can taste what remains of myself on her lips.

Happiness seems to fill me, sending my heart rate soaring as the feeling intensifies. It's frightening and exhilarating at the same time. Bringing me to the realisation that

I have no fucking idea what I'm doing or how the fuck I'm going to stop this. Because no matter how hard I try, I keep coming back for more.

CHAPTER 16

Lauren

As we lie in bed, coming down from our high, my head is resting on his chest. He has an arm around me, his fingers slowly tracing circles on my arm, my skin tingling from his touch.

"Tell me something about yourself that I don't already know," he says.

"You know everything there is to know. You know where I work, where I live. I'm just a regular twenty-eight-year-old with regular dreams and aspirations."

"And what are those dreams and aspirations?"

"Same as everyone else, I guess. To do well, succeed in my job. Maybe one day get married and have a family."

His fingers instantly freeze. I feel his chest rise and fall as he draws in a breath, and his body shifts slightly, as if he wants to pull away.

"Relax, stud. I'm a realist. I had the memo. I know you're not looking for anything long term." *Do I? Do I? Then why do I keep coming back for more?*

"You know, Adam warned me off you. Said you're not like the usual women I go for."

I turn on my side to look at him with raised eyebrows

at his unexpected comment. "What's that supposed to mean?"

He lifts his shoulder in a half shrug. "You're Jules's best friend. I suppose he's worried I'll hurt you."

I lift my head to study his face. His eyes are indifferent as they glance around the room. They look anywhere and everywhere except at me.

"Are you going to hurt me?" My voice is soft, belying the fact that the mere thought of it is tearing at my insides, even though I know, at the back of my mind, that's what's going to happen.

This question seems to warrant his attention, and he pushes himself onto his side and props himself up on his forearm to look at me. His dark brown eyes soften as they stare into mine. Then featherlike laugh lines crinkle around his eyes and there's a trace of laughter in his voice.

"Only if you fall madly in love with me." A devilish look enters his eyes as he winks at me.

Heed the warning, says the voice in my head. But it's like closing the stable door after the horse has bolted; too late for precautions, too late to safeguard my heart.

"What sort of women do you usually go for?"

He sighs, lies back down, and puts his hands behind his head, his eyes focusing on the ceiling again.

"Women devoid of any scruples. Eager women. Sex on the first date kind of women. I've also had sex with plenty of women without a date."

"So basically, you're dissing women for liking sex instead of being repulsed by it. For being in control of their bodies, for being sexually aware, and being able to decide if they want sex or not. We had sex without dating, does that make me easy?"

"You're getting worked up unnecessarily. You're kind of

ruining the moment here. Did I say I thought that about you?"

I snap at him. "No, but it's implied." I push myself upright and catapult myself out of the bed. "I don't know what I was thinking at the wedding, fucking the groomsman. Jesus, it's the total opposite of not shitting where you eat. I'm such an idiot. And you didn't even have to buy me a drink, let alone take me out to dinner. Why would you respect me after I slept with you so quickly?"

"Lauren, stop." He sits up, grabs my arm before I can get away, and swings me around to face him, pulling me between his thighs as he sits on the edge of the bed, holding me tightly by both my arms as his dick presses against my stomach.

"I didn't mean it like that. It's just that there are women who only care about snagging a guy for an easy ride, and that's fine. And if a guy is happy with that, that's fine too, it's their choice."

I huff out a breath before speaking. "For the record, I love my life. I love my job. I'm happy living in my tiny one-bedroom apartment. It may not be as plush and in a trendy upmarket area like yours, but it's mine. I purchased it all on my own. I pay my own mortgage. I don't need a man to succeed, and I certainly don't need a man to make me happy." *Except you. I want you.* "And unless it's escaped your notice, women don't even need a man to have an orgasm. There are toys for that."

"You're angry. Please calm down." His voice is measured and controlled.

"I'm not angry. I'm disappointed. You have some antiquated view of women, and I don't like it. As a matter of fact, I'd say you're the easy one. Always too eager and ready. Always too willing. I just need to click my fingers, and you'll come running, happy to put out. Have you ever thought about that? Hmm. Hmm. No, because you're a man, and it's different for men."

"Sit down and listen for once." He pulls me onto his lap, his arms holding me tight and close to him, making it all the more difficult for me to fight my corner, let alone my own desire at the feeling of his hardness against my body.

"I wasn't criticising. What I meant is, that yes, I do avail myself of these women because it suits me at this point in my life. I have other priorities, so dating is not my first concern at the moment. I don't want conversations about the future. I can't get emotionally attached because my energies are focused elsewhere right now."

"Thanks for the reminder." I lower my head and find myself staring at his bare feet. He has nice feet. They look smooth and all his toes go in a line down from his big toe to his little toe. His toenails are perfectly trimmed. Does he have pedicures?

I start to wonder if there's anything about this man that isn't perfect? Oh, yeah, his lack of commitment.

Then as if on cue, the entire sequence of yesterday's events come flooding back in full Technicolor. *Are you forgetting the woman who was here yesterday?* How the fuck could I forget about that? Surely I wasn't that drunk? Did I deliberately ignore the evidence so I could have sex without the guilt trip afterwards?

If it were anyone else, I would ask, *how stupid can you be?* And that they'd be an idiot to put themselves through this. But it doesn't matter how many times I tell myself not to, or how many times I try and impose some self-discipline, I struggle to control myself where he's concerned. He's like a drug. And I need my medication before the withdrawal symptoms become too intense.

As I lift my head, his arms remain wrapped around my waist, and my eyes are drawn to his tattoo.

The question is lingering on the tip of my tongue. Do I really want to know? Second thoughts poke at me like a sharp knife. But I've been living in cuckoo land, pretending I don't know she exists. Even if the amnesia was alcohol induced, the fact that I've been foolish enough to sleep with him again after coming face to face with Rose has got to make me the most dim-witted female on the planet.

I straighten up, tuck a lock of hair behind my ear. There's only a microsecond of hesitation before I speak. "Does this have anything to do with Rose?"

His hold on me loosens. I notice the tension in his firm-set jaw as his eyes widen in astonishment. Is it because I've dared to ask about her again? I won't be fobbed off this time. I won't allow myself to be distracted. I need to call on every ounce of backbone to face this head-on.

He remains silent, but I continue on the topic, fully aware that I may not like what I hear. "I don't know very much of anything except her name, and that she exists. Even my best friend wouldn't break your confidence, so you should feel pretty proud of yourself. But thanks to Susanna, as limited as it is, she took such delight in divulging the information. So when I saw you leave the bar with that woman on Friday, I needed to come and see for myself whether or not she stayed the weekend. I was expecting to find you together. Instead I had a very brief conversation at your apartment door with another woman. You seem to like spreading yourself around.

"So, who is she? Obviously from what you've just said she's not a girlfriend. She's a little too young to be your secretary or another man's wife. An intern? Is it a friends-with-benefits situation? Oh my God, is it a friend's daughter? Are you in love with her? Spit it out."

My heart is pounding in my chest as I'm spewing verbal diarrhoea. Because as much as I want to know, somehow I don't.

There's a hint of annoyance in his voice but his tone remains even. "The woman you saw me with on Friday is a client. And contrary to what you may think, I can separate business and pleasure.

"With regards to Rose, yes, I love her. She's my world. She's the most beautiful, sweetest woman I've ever known. No one else will ever compare to how I feel about her. I don't think I could ever love anyone as much as I love her."

Tears glisten in my eyes as he talks about another woman with the words I so desperately hoped he would eventually to say to me.

I've finally run out of steam. I feel drained. The energy in my body depleted. I resign myself to the realization of what he's just said, and what this means for my delusional hopes of an us—of a future with him.

I free myself from his clutches and stand up. "If you're so in love with another woman, why isn't she here? Why am I here? Why aren't you with her?"

He seems amused by my reaction. A smile actually permeates his face. Is he mocking me? I'm about to tell him to shove it up his you know what, but he starts blabbing with such enthusiasm.

"I love her more than anything, but she's also a pain in the butt—she's head strong—doesn't listen to a word I say—thinks she knows everything, and never does what she's told. You could say you have that in common."

"Gee, thanks for the compliment. Am I supposed to be

grateful that you speak of me in the same breath as her? Is that meant to make me feel flattered?" I continue to locate my clothes so I can get dressed and maybe get out of here with a hint of dignity still intact. I really don't want to listen to his preoccupation with another woman.

He stands up and grabs my arm. "Lauren, please stop. You don't understand."

I shake my arm free. "I understand perfectly. You've been fucking me while you're in love with someone else. Even if you're not having sex with her, it's still cheating. Especially if she feels the same about you. I can't believe I've managed to get myself into this position again. What's worse is, this time I've done it willingly. I ignored my instincts. I made excuses for your behaviour. I pretended the signs weren't there. I followed my heart because I thought we had something. I thought you just needed time. But you've been playing me all along."

He seems to take offence to this. He grabs both my arms. "I've never lied to you."

"Ever heard the phrase lying by omission? Now let go of me."

"No, not until you calm down."

"I am calm. Believe me, you don't want to see the alternative, it involves you getting physically hurt. Now I've got the whole picture everything is perfectly clear. I'm stepping aside so you can go do whatever it is you want to do with Rose. Fuck her every which way. Fuck her hard and fast. Fuck her into oblivion for all I care. Make her scream your name as she comes. Give her multiple orgasms. Trust me, she'll love you for it, and you'll have her coming back more. She'll be begging you for it." I hurl my words at him like stones.

He's holding my arms, it's almost as if he's using all of

his willpower to not shake me. Shock at my words have him shouting at me. "Goddamn it, will you stop talking about her like that. It's sickening."

I shout back. "Why should I? Why is she so special? Why her and not me? What makes her so different to all the others, to me? I want to know. I deserve to know."

The sudden sound of his voice as it booms around the room surprises me, but it's what he says that causes me to take a gasp of breath in absolute shock.

"Because Rose is my fifteen-year-old daughter."

I feel my whole body slump as he releases my arms from his grip. I stare at him, speechless. The breath I've just taken is caught in my lungs.

I watch as he rakes a hand through his hair, taking a moment to compose himself, giving me an opportunity to absorb the magnitude of what he's just told me.

He sits on the edge of the bed, hunched over, resting his arms on his thighs, lacing his fingers together as he stares at the ground.

His voice drops in volume. "Aren't you going to say anything?"

"I'm not sure what to say. This is so… not what I was expecting at all."

"What were you expecting? By the look on your face, it seems you'd be happier if I were actually seeing another woman?"

"No, that's not it at all. I suppose it's the fact that you've managed to keep it a secret. That's what's shocked me. When were you going to introduce me to her?"

"I wasn't."

Ouch. "May I ask why not?"

"That part of my life has nothing to do with us. It's separate from us."

"Us? Don't make me laugh. I opened myself up for you. I let you in. But you've been keeping me at arm's length the whole time. So don't brand the word around as if this is anything other than you and me having sex."

He straightens up and reaches out to take my hand. "Come and sit down."

I allow him to gently pull me towards him, and I drop down on the bed beside him, conscious of the fact that we're both still stark naked.

I glance at him, unable to fathom the reason why he would in effect hide from me the fact that he has a daughter.

He lets go of my hand, whips his head around to look at me. His eyes are dark and wild as he toys with a lock of my hair.

"Beautiful, Lauren."

When he leans in to kiss me, I put a hand on his chest and hold him back. "What are you doing?"

He stares back at me, his eyes almost imploring me for understanding as he sweeps his fingers up and down my arm, causing my skin to tingle and my pulse to quicken.

"What does it look like? More importantly, what does it feel like?" His voice is husky and authoritative.

Perhaps I'm being naïve, foolish even, for wanting him so much right now. But I will not allow my emotions, or his galvanising look, melt away my resolve. I want answers. I've been pretending for long enough. He hasn't made a fool of me; I've managed to do that all on my own, and I refuse to stick my head in the sand any longer.

"Why would you keep the fact that you have a daughter a secret?"

I guess that's the question that breaks the camel's back as he replies snappily, "What the fuck in this scenario aren't you getting?"

I push myself up from the bed, grab my dress, and slip it over my head, then make my way to the living room, I'll locate my underwear later.

"Where are you going?" He stands, puts on a pair of sweatpants, and follows me.

"We are not having this conversation whilst horizontal."

"What makes you think we're having this conversation at all?"

"For crying out loud, you can't just drop a bombshell of this magnitude and expect me to ignore it and not even discuss it. You can't expect to shut me up with sex like you usually do. It won't work this time if that's what you're trying to do?"

"Do you want an answer to that or is it a rhetorical question?" There's almost a smirk on his face, as if he's enjoying this whole performance and gaining some perverse pleasure from my turmoil.

I meet his eyes without flinching. "Are you going to stop acting like an arsehole and actually have an adult conversation about this."

"Oh, I don't know, what's there to talk about." He makes his way towards the kitchen. "Coffee?"

I follow hot on his heels. He slips a pod into the coffee machine and grabs the milk from the fridge. Acting as though everything is normal.

"I know what you're doing."

"Pretty obvious I'm making coffee."

"Stop being a clever clogs. It's becoming tiresome."

He leans against the counter and crosses his arms. "What is it I'm doing that has you so riled up?"

"This." I gesture with my hand in a circular motion

in his direction. "You're nonchalant attitude to this situation. You have a daughter. A fact that you've managed to keep from me for two whole months. I want to know why?"

He turns to the coffee machine and swaps over the cups, handing me the coffee he's just made after adding milk. He pauses, as though he's taking a moment to reflect. Once his coffee is ready, he takes the cup and comes to stand next to me at the island counter.

"I've already explained to you that I have other priorities, or has the sex and multiple orgasms fogged your brain and made you forget our conversation already?"

"That was out of context because it was before I knew you had a daughter. And just to clarify, it was one orgasm. You must be losing your touch."

He places his cup down and silently moves closer to me, an invitation very evident in the depths of his smouldering eyes as he aligns his body with mine, placing his hands on the countertop either side of me, boxing me in, his desire pressing against my hip. "I can rectify that if you like."

"Can't you be serious for two minutes?"

"I'm being perfectly serious. Nothing's changed. This doesn't have to interfere with us and what we're doing."

"What are we doing exactly?"

He waggles his brows. "Well, if you need me to draw you a picture, maybe I haven't been doing it right."

There's several seconds of silence as his dark eyes glow with an expectancy. I force myself to stay on track. Determined not be distracted by him, I speak calmly but firmly.

"I'd like to meet her, properly I mean."

He stiffens at the request, sighing loudly as he pulls away, in effect putting me at arm's length. He takes his cup and places it in the sink, and with his back to me he says, "I'm not sure that's a good idea."

"Why not? What do you think is going to happen?"

He's standing with his hands gripping the edge of the counter, motionless except for the rise and fall of his shoulders as he shrugs.

"Please turn around and look at me."

When he spins around, he hesitates a moment before saying anything. "What's to be gained by you meeting Rose? I've spent the last fifteen years making sure I don't traipse every woman I'm sleeping with through her life."

His reluctance has me second guessing this whole situation. What is the point? I suspect it's because it would make me feel emotionally closer to him. Something he obviously doesn't want.

"It's not a question of gaining anything. This relationship means something to me. You mean something to me. As much as you want to pretend otherwise, you're caring and gentle, and I want to see that side of you with your daughter. I want to know Mark Taylor the father. I suppose I want something that goes beyond just the physical. I know you have feelings for me, otherwise why come to the bar when Sam called you? You said you cared about me. Why won't you give in to how you feel?"

He steps towards me, stopping in front of me. I can see the moment his apprehension starts to slowly dissipate, as his eyes hold mine, gentle and contemplative, drinking me in. He gives me a warm, dreamy smile and nods.

I feel a warm glow flow through me, but I don't have time to bask in my blissfully happy state, as his hands take my face, holding it gently as he leans in. When our lips meet, I instantly melt at the tender affection coming from him and wrap my arms around his neck, throwing everything into this kiss so that he will know, without any words being spoken, that I love him.

CHAPTER 17
Mark

I must have been deluded if I thought getting Rose on board was going to be a walk in the park. How can a fifteen-year-old give you so much attitude yet still seem indifferent I'll never know.

"You mean the weirdo?" She brings a hand up to stifle her laughter. For some inexplicable reason, she seems to find this whole situation hilarious.

I shoot her a stern look of warning. "I would appreciate it if you didn't refer to Lauren in that way. She is not a weirdo. For your information she's intelligent, kind, gentle—"

She rolls her eyes at me. "Dad, you can stop with the résumé. Must be serious then if you want me to officially meet her?"

"Actually, it was her suggestion."

"Yes, Dad, but you're going along with it. You never have with other women. Why give in to this one?"

"Because I like her—a lot."

"Are you going to marry her? Is she going to be my wicked stepmother?"

"Let's not get ahead of ourselves. We're barely dating.

Just make sure you're on your best behaviour when you do meet."

"Okay, Dad, it's your funeral." She gives a shrug as she puts her headphones back on and saunters off to her room, seeming to take all of this in her stride, thankfully.

I, on the other hand, am feeling a little apprehensive. I relax back into the sofa, contemplating whether I've done the right thing. I guess it remains to be seen. But I couldn't help myself. It wasn't just her determination and the fact that she was so persistent. It was when I could see the twinge of disappointment etched on her face that I finally realised that if I didn't do this, I would lose her, we'd be over, and I'm not ready for us to be over yet. I've tried to distance myself. I've tried to give the impression that I don't give a shit about her. But it's not working. I want to give her more. I want to take more. And if meeting Rose is what she wants, that's what will happen. What's a little compromise to keep a woman happy, and for some puzzling reason, I want to make Lauren happy.

I'll readily admit I'm not the kind of guy to leave cute notes. The only time I send flowers are for a funeral or my mother's birthday—a rule I've already broken for Lauren.

Sexting I can do, but don't expect sweet, romantic messages. All I offer is sex, and I know exactly how to keep Lauren happy in the bedroom. I like taking my time. I pay attention to her needs, asking her what she wants, how she wants it. I explore the different erogenous zones of her body with a light feathery touch here, a gentle kiss there. Sometimes slow and easy, others, hard and fast. And as much as I'm able to keep her happy sexually, she gives it back tenfold. I don't think I've ever had such an emotional connection with a woman, not even Rose's mother. It's as though she's awakened something within me that I never realised I was holding back. A contentment—an intense feeling of peace—and I like that feeling. I want to feel it with Lauren. I want to continue feeling it for as long as possible.

I know she sees me as social and outgoing with plenty of options when it comes to female company. They say actions speak louder than words, so this is me letting her know without words how much she means to me. This is me showing her that she's the only woman who matters to me. Maybe subconsciously it's me who wants more. Well fuck me if that's not a scary thought.

So even though this compromise may seem small to her, for me it's huge, and whilst I know unequivocally that I keep her satisfied when it comes to sex, for the first time in my life, I don't feel that's enough. And for the first time in my life, I'm considering having a serious relationship.

If truth be known, I think Lauren could be a good role model for Rose. Granted, her mother and I do our best to instil decent morals, but it's a well-known fact that teenagers do not want to listen to advice from their parents. So yes, be it selfish of me, I have a multitude of ulterior motives. I just hope that I'm not going to live to regret my decision.

CHAPTER 18

Lauren

Never in a million years did I think he would agree to my meeting Rose. He hadn't mentioned our discussion at all over the week that followed, and I felt I'd said and done enough on the subject. I was ready to throw in the towel. Walk away broken-hearted.

So, it was completely unexpected when he informed me that he'd arranged a lunch date for the three of us. He's kept it low key, a burger place on the high street.

I recognise this is huge for him. And the fact that it's happening at all tells me that I do mean something to him. He has feelings for me. Even if he's too stubborn to admit it.

Of course I'm nervous as to whether she'll like me. I wouldn't be human if I weren't. Will she feel threatened? Will she think I'm trying to take her mother's place? Will she resent me for taking up her father's time, time that could be spent with her?

I do my best to mentally prepare myself. But I remind myself that there's only so much I can do to ensure that this meeting goes smoothly. And even though I'm going in with a positive attitude, I also need to be realistic in my expectations.

I need to ensure that displays of affection between myself and Mark are limited, preferably to zero, this is not about Mark and me.

Although her greeting is informal, a slight wave of the hand, it comes as no surprise that she's guarded at first. But she loosens up after a while, becoming more comfortable by the minute when I'm able to engage her in conversation about the latest movies and upcoming music festivals. My suggestion that perhaps I can take her and a friend to one in the future is met with the obligatory one shoulder shrug of indifference, not wanting to give anything away.

Mark's face is a picture as the lines of concentration deepen along his brows, and he can't hide his nervousness as it flits across his handsome face. It's a new look for him. I'm guessing it's a feeling he's never known or experienced before.

It's only when Rose tells him to relax and chill out that I notice the tension in his shoulders ease, and he finally sits back comfortably, his confidence coming back as he seems reassured by her words.

No matter how much I tell myself to slow down, to not allow myself to become too invested, it's of no use, I already am. Obviously, this makes me want to get to know Rose. Find out her likes and dislikes. I'm sure if I Google it, there are plenty of do-and-don't articles about how to get to know your boyfriend's children.

With this in mind, I decide it would be fun to spend the day together, just Rose and me. A chance for us to spend some quality time getting to know each other a little better. Show her that I'm not the Wicked Witch of the West, and that I'm not here to come between her and her father. I don't expect her to welcome me instantly into the bosom of their family unit. I'm not looking to take the place of a mother figure; her mother is very much alive and kicking. The plan is to slowly but surely get to know her, and for her to get to know me, by doing something fun, and hopefully she'll like me.

And what else does a fifteen-year-old love to do more than shop. So, armed with my credit card, Rose and I are going to spend Saturday afternoon splashing the cash to help boost the economy. To be honest, I'm looking forward to it myself. I've been so busy with work lately that it's been a while since I've ventured to the shops for a shopping spree. Maybe I could buy some sexy lingerie that Mark will appreciate.

We'd agreed to meet at Westfield Shopping Mall in west London, and I'm sitting in a coffee shop, strumming my fingers on the table—it's the waiting—the fear of the unknown. The prospect of our first interaction without Mark. Will she give me a major dose of attitude now that Mark won't be with us to act as a buffer? Or will she simply be indifferent?

All manner of feelings are at the forefront. I won't say I'm not nervous, just not as nervous today; it's a mixture of excitement and optimism, a hopefulness about the future and what this could mean for my relationship with Mark. You could say everything is riding on how Rose takes to me.

It was difficult to gauge anything from our first meeting. Whilst it seemed to go okay, for all I know it could have been for show. Maybe she was being pleasant to appease her father. Maybe today she'll be the teenage brat from hell.

I sit in the chair, one leg crossed over the other gently

swinging back and forth restlessly. In fact, if I could have a cigarette right now, that would really calm my nerves. But I don't smoke. And do I really want to greet Rose while a nicotine stick is dangling between my lips? Tight deadlines and the nervous energy I feel before boardroom meetings with clients are nothing compared to this.

Each time the door opens I look up in anticipation. I'm not sure what to label this. Just two friends getting together for a girlie day out. And what will it mean for my relationship with Mark if Rose doesn't take to me? Nonetheless, I remind myself not to try too hard. Nothing screams desperation more than trying to be a people pleaser.

When I first suggested a day out, she was speechless, she thought it was a joke, so much so that she actually let out a small laugh. But when I didn't laugh with her, that's when she realised I was serious.

I may have scored double points with Mark as he sat back and watched the exchange, while suppressing his amusement. But when Rose agreed, he was unable to hide his satisfaction. He winked at me and rewarded me with a smile that sent my pulse racing.

I've never had to consider dating a guy with children, probably because I've never dated anyone older. I've always dated men my own age or no more than a couple of years older. It's never been a conscious decision, just how it is. But I really do want to make it work with Mark, and his agreeing to let me meet her surely means that he wants that too.

Rose does seem like a good kid, even if she does appear to be a little cautious about me. I can understand that. She's been the apple of her father's eye for fifteen years without interruption or distraction. And from what

I now know, he's never had what constitutes a proper relationship. He's never dated seriously. He's always kept women at arm's length, always putting Rose first.

My attention darts to the door as it opens again, and finally, Rose strolls in wearing skinny jeans, T-shirt, pink Converse, and a leather biker jacket. She has a small leather fashionable rucksack slung over one shoulder. Unlike our lunch date, her black hair is left loose today and tumbling past her shoulders. It's parted in the centre, and her bangs fall just below her eyebrows, adding to the rock-chic look.

She's looking around until she spots me, and I'm pleased that when she does, the corners of her mouth curve into a smile as she walks towards me.

"Hey, Lauren, are you ready to shop till you drop?"

I flash her a warm but competitive smile as I grab my tote bag and stand. "Please, I invented the phrase. Watch and learn, Rose, watch and learn." We head out of the coffee shop with Rose eagerly following along behind me.

It turns out that there's an ulterior motive for accepting today's invitation, and he goes by the name of Dan. She has a thing for a guy at school and wants to make an effort to impress him. Of course, I go through the reasoning of not changing yourself for anyone, staying true to yourself, but we've all been there, so I do my best to help her in her choice of outfits, consciously steering clear of anything too revealing.

After four hours, one break at a juice bar to grab a drink and a sandwich, a make-up tutorial at the Chanel counter, and laden with bags of clothes, shoes, and make-up, we're headed home in a cab when Mark calls Rose.

She rolls her eyes. "Yes, Dad. Okay, Dad. I will."

As I listen to Rose's short replies to his questions, it

does make me wonder how he managed to stop himself calling earlier. Perhaps he didn't want to add any pressure to the situation. Maybe it was pride. I smile to myself as I imagine him anxiously pacing back and forth in his apartment while he wonders what we're up to and how we're getting on.

After a brief conversation, she hands the phone to me. Mark's voice is low and smooth in my ear, causing a tingle of excitement inside me. When he invites me to have an early dinner with them at home, it makes my heart sing with delight, and I happily accept.

As we sit in the back of the cab for the remainder of the ride, I reflect on my day with Rose. I'm filled with satisfaction at the fact she and I have been able to have so much fun together. Hopefully, it's not a one-off, and I've even been able to penetrate the wall she has up.

CHAPTER 19

Lauren

Dinner consists of takeout Chinese and a three-way squabble as to who will have the last remaining spring roll. Mark and I relent, and Rose takes great pleasure in her triumph, taunting us in good humour with her victory dance.

Having finished our meal, and after helping Mark load the dishwasher, I sit on one of the two-seater sofa's while Mark sits opposite me on the other. Rose sits on the floor, her back leaning against the sofa where Mark sits, her legs stretched casually before her as she scrolls through her phone doing a roll call for Mark of all her friends that she wants to invite to her forthcoming birthday celebrations.

I feel like a spare tyre as I listen to them making plans for her sixteenth birthday. Plans, I hasten to add, that do not seem to include me. I contemplate contributing to the conversation with some ideas but think better of it. I can see how much they're engrossed in their conversation, so I sit in silence.

I don't know if I'm jealous or simply disappointed that he'll be celebrating Rose's birthday with her and her mother. That's perfectly natural. It's refreshing to see two separated parents actually agreeing and getting on. What I'm disheartened about is that I don't figure anywhere in any of their plans. Not even a separate dinner for the three of us. Maybe I expect too much too soon. Perhaps today didn't go as well as I thought. Maybe I've read too much into things again. That seems to be my default setting.

The reality of the situation is that I don't fit in to this part of his life. Rose is his priority, as she should be, he's always made that clear, but it still hurts. Because as the days and weeks pass, my feelings for Mark have escalated to the point of no return.

I'm counting up all these things and adding them to the list of cons. I actually believed that my meeting Rose meant that he's willing to find room for me, and we could spend more time together, have a regular relationship. But I have to face facts. The only reason he relented and allowed me to meet Rose is because he wants to continue having sex with me.

I suppose I should take it as a compliment, as I'm sure there's no shortage of women desperate to be in his bed.

I do my best to clear my head of these thoughts and focus back on their conversation.

"Do you think Mum will let me go to a club? Can I have two celebrations, one with you and Mum and one with my friends?"

"You can do whatever you want, except going to a club. You're too young."

Don't ask me why, but for some inexplicable reason, this is the moment I decide to add my two cents worth. "I went to a club for my sixteenth."

There's a significant lifting of his brows. "Considering the legal age is eighteen, I dread to think how you managed that. In any event, that's not the sort of thing I want for my daughter at sixteen."

I'm not entirely sure if it's what he said or how he said it. His voice seems to have an accusatory tone to it. I boldly meet his eyes and respond sharply. "What's that supposed to mean?"

There's no humour in his smile as he looks at me, his brows shooting up in surprise at my defensive tone. "Nothing. I just don't want a daughter of mine frequenting night clubs. Next thing we know she'll have a boyfriend."

"Oh my God!" shrieks Rose as she jumps to her feet. "You're such a dinosaur. All my friends have boyfriends."

"Perhaps you shouldn't be associating with these friends. Maybe they're a bad influence."

I can't help it, I'm unable to keep my thoughts to myself. Probably because I know what it's like to be the odd one out amongst my school friends. "That's a little overprotective, don't you think?" I say.

"She's fifteen," he says in defiance.

"She'll be sixteen in a few weeks."

"She doesn't need a boyfriend. What she needs to be doing is focusing on her studies. That's where her priorities should be if she wants to go to university," he adds.

I resolve to try and help them find a happy medium and suddenly remember the joint campaign launch Jules did for Rivera Jewellery and King's Golden scotch. "What about hiring a venue with a DJ? A rooftop bar perhaps?"

Rose sits next to her father, shoulder to shoulder, and puts on a soft, sugary-sweet voice, which I'm in no doubt always gets her what she wants. Perhaps I could learn a thing or two from this kid.

"Oh, Dad, I like that Idea, please can we do that? Lauren

will help, won't you?" She glances over at me with pleading eyes.

I try to hide my happiness at the fact that she's now including me in her plans. "Of course. I'd love to help if your dad doesn't mind."

There's a significant lifting of his brows and a shake of his head, as the last traces of resistance vanish when his mouth curves into a smile. "I suppose I'm not going to win this one, am I? Okay, I'll talk to your mother. She'll probably want to help with the organising. You know what she's like. We don't need to take up Lauren's time."

And there you have it. The door firmly shut in my face. They're a family. I'm an outsider. It seems I've completely misread this situation—it appears that Rose isn't the one keeping me at arm's length.

As if that isn't enough to make me realise that perhaps things with Mark aren't moving forward in the way I'd hoped, the final nail in the coffin comes when I get a phone call four days later. And what happens as a consequence of that call seals my fate.

The caller ID says *private number.* I momentarily hesitate in answering it in case it's Andrew or his soon-to-be ex-wife. But I quickly dismiss such a notion. I haven't heard a peep from either of them since Mark dealt with that whole sorry mess.

"Hello," I answer to the sound of muffled sobs.

"It's me, Rose."

"Rose?" I'm unable to hide my surprise. I haven't seen Mark since the three of us had dinner at his place. He's called me, he's told me he's been busy with work. He's called me at night too, just to say goodnight. You don't do that with a casual hook up, so I'm taking it as a good sign —it's progress.

But Rose calling me sobbing down the phone has me worried. And then a disturbing thought has me even more concerned.

"What on earth is wrong? Is your dad okay? Has something happened to him?"

Her sobs are almost choking her, so much so that fear sweeps through me. I do my best to project a deceptive calmness in my voice.

"Rose, you need to take a deep breath and tell me what's wrong. I can't help if you don't tell me."

She can just about manage to speak through her sobs. "I've done something really stupid and awful. I'm too scared to tell my dad. I'm in so much trouble. He'll kill me if he finds out. Please, you have to help me."

"Okay, calm down. Of course I'll help you. First, you need to tell me where you are. I'll come and meet you right now."

"I'm outside."

"Outside? You mean outside my apartment building?" I head to the living room window, and yep, sure enough there she is standing at the main entrance, shoulders hunched as she looks around nervously, hoodie up as if to hide her identity. Jesus Christ, I can't even begin to fathom what this is about. Rather than buzz her in, I put my apartment door on the latch and hastily head down to the main door to greet her.

When I open the door, she's standing there looking so frightened and fragile. Her eyes are red and puffy from crying. I instinctively put my arm around her shoulder as I escort her to my apartment, where I guide her to the sofa and she sits, very still, her head bowed.

"Would you like a drink of water? I have juice if you prefer."

She shakes her head as she pushes the hood off, then brushes her hair away from her face with her hand. There's a deafening silence. Mindful of her vulnerability, I lower my voice to a soft gentle tone, ready to take the bull by the horns, as I sit next her, close enough to put my arm around her if necessary.

"Do you want to tell me what's brought you to my doorstep?"

She lifts her head to look at me. Her eyes fly open as the panic sets in. "You have to promise not to tell my dad."

"I'm not sure—"

A shadow of alarm sweeps across her face as fear takes hold. "No, please. If you don't promise I won't tell you."

I place a hand over both of hers, which she's nervously wringing in her lap "Okay, sweetie, I promise."

A tense silence looms as she takes a deep breath. "There's a boy at school."

I should have known. "Are you talking about Dan?"

She nods as she wipes the tears away from her cheeks with her sleeve, prompting me to fetch a box of tissues and place them on the coffee table in front of her.

"He said he liked me. I was thinking I would ask him to my party, and we've been texting for a couple of weeks. But then he asked me for a picture."

Oh dear God. Please don't let this be what I think it is. I try not to stir uneasily in my seat. I do my best to stay calm and focused. I pause for a moment to take a subtle breath before I choose my words carefully.

"What kind of picture?" I know the answer even before I finish asking the question. She proceeds to scroll through her phone to access her photos. Her cheeks colour, and her embarrassment makes her hesitate a fraction before she holds her phone up in front of me so I can see for myself.

Yep, just as I thought. Boob pic.

While I'm outwardly calm, below the surface there's only one thought going through my mind. What will Mark's reaction be?

I focus on Rose. She looks so frightened, so anxious. "Did he send you any photos?"

Swallowing a sob languishing in her throat, she looks up and shakes her head. Thank God for small mercies.

How do I handle this? The only experience I have is that I was once a fifteen-year-old. But I do know that right now is not the time to lecture her about the consequences of sexting, so I try to keep it to a minimum.

"Okay, this isn't an ideal situation, but perhaps it's not as bad as you think it is. Looking from the outside in, every girl wants to feel special. Every girl wants the boy she likes to like her back, and sometimes, we do foolish things. Everyone makes mistakes. It's all part of growing up. What made you send the photo?"

Her head is bowed again in embarrassment, her body slumped. "It's so stupid. He said if he liked the look of my tits, I could be his girlfriend. I can't believe I'm so pathetic to fall for it."

I lightly push a strand of hair away from her cheek, and she lifts her head to look at me.

"Hey, it's not pathetic. You mustn't think like that, okay. But lesson number one: If a guy ever puts those sorts of conditions on you, throw him to the kerb.

"Lesson number two: You need to be a little savvier when a boy gives you some attention. Act like he's not so special, and you get attention all the time. That way he'll work harder. And never, ever, feel peer pressured into doing anything you don't want to do, especially just to be in with the 'in-crowd.' You are in control, not some spotty, horny teenage boy or the popular girls at school."

As she listens intently, the tears have stopped, and she's nodding, taking in everything I'm saying. But she looks so delicate that I instinctively sweep her into my arms and hold her there, hugging her, only letting go when I feel the tension gradually ease from her body.

"Are you feeling any better?"

She's leaning into me lightly, perhaps as some form of comfort. "Yes, a little. Thanks."

"Haven't your parents ever talked about boys with you?"

"Not really. I don't think Dad knows how to broach the subject. I think he's hoping I don't grow up, so he doesn't have to deal with it. We've had the mandatory RSE at school."

My confused expression is obviously evident as she proceeds to clarify. "Relationship and Sex Education. My mum's going to be so annoyed with me. She's always going on about how to be prim and proper and act like a lady, be respectful. What's she going to say when she finds out that I can't even respect myself? They're both going to hit the roof. I can kiss goodbye to having a party for my birthday."

"I don't think you're giving your dad enough credit. I haven't met your mum, but I'm sure she'll be supportive, they both will. You'll see. Would you like me to take you home?"

"Could you? You won't tell my dad, will you?"

"I made you a promise. But in all honesty, I do think you should tell him. He may want to speak to the school, ask them to contact the boy's parents, and get him to delete the photo."

"Oh my God, No! That would be so humiliating. Can't we just keep it a secret?"

I don't want to alarm her any further by telling her these things never stay secret for very long. "What about your mum? Maybe you could talk to her?"

"They always stick together. She's almost as bad as my dad."

We sit in silence in the cab on the way to Mark's apartment. I stupidly assumed I was doing the right thing in advising Rose to come clean and speak to her dad. I know Mark can be overprotective when it comes to his daughter, but I never thought that I'd be the one on the receiving end of his anger.

CHAPTER 20
Lauren

After taking my advice and deciding that it would be best to come clean, Rose asks me to go inside with her and stay for moral support while she confesses to her father, and I duly oblige. I'm sitting in silence as she tearfully recounts her story, word for word, as we'd discussed earlier.

Mark, for his part, manages to stay calm. Sitting back silently on the sofa, one leg crossed over the other, one arm casually placed on the armrest. Not one flicker of a reaction. Allowing her to finish without interruption. When she's done, he stands up and instructs her to go to her room, seemingly unmoved by her tears.

"But Dad—"

"No buts. Do as your told."

Her shoulders sag as she looks at me and gives a tentative smile, her forehead creasing with concern. I return her smile with one of my own, letting her know I'm proud of her before she walks off in a huff, closing her bedroom door a little more forcefully than necessary.

And that's the moment he turns on me. He keeps his voice low, but the bridled anger is still present. His eyes flash with anger, his voice cold and reprimanding as he doesn't hold back.

"What makes you think you have the right to counsel my daughter? You are not her mother. In case you need reminding, she has a mother."

This is certainly not what I expected. I expected him to be grateful. I expected him at the very least to thank me for being there for his daughter in her hour of need.

The shock of his reaction surprises me as I wonder why on earth he's coming down on me so hard. My own anger and hurt forces me out of my seat, and I snap back at him in frustration.

"She came to me for help. She was beside herself. What would you have me do? Turn my back on her? Do you have any idea how much courage it took for her to come to you and tell you all of this? She was so frightened about how you'd react, and now I can see she was justified in her assumptions."

"I'm not going to argue my point. If it's a choice, there isn't one. It's always going to be my daughter. She'll always come first."

The bluntness of his words hit me full force, my anger making me retaliate, not caring how it sounds, not caring that my voice is now raised.

"How fucking dare you. Don't you think I know that? Rose is your little girl and will forever be your little girl, but she's also a grown woman. All I've ever wanted was for you to make a little more time for me in your life. I've never once asked you to choose. But you know what, I'm going to choose for you. I want to be someone's everything. I want to be the one who is put first. That's what I deserve. I don't want to be the fuck of the month. I don't want to be the optional add-on when there's no other alternative. And the fact that you won't do that for me speaks volumes."

His voice is uncompromising, his words harsh and accusing. "Since you don't have children of your own, you can't possibly understand what being a parent is about or what it involves. There's a clear boundary here, and you've crossed it."

His words cut through me like a knife as they stab at my heart. I blink away the tears threatening to escape as I swallow the lump lingering in my throat, but I manage to choke out my words.

"Oh, wow! Please, accept my apologies for the fact that every guy I've ever met has screwed me over in one way or another. I guess I can now add you to that list.

"I've tried to make good choices, but I've only ever met shitty men. So I'm sorry I've never met a decent man to fall in love with me and sweep me off my feet. I'm sorry I don't know where I'm supposed to find a man to love me enough to have children with me and perhaps even marry me. I'm sorry if it's my fault that I'm not a parent and can't relate to what you must be going through. But you know what, you don't have a monopoly on fatherhood. So fuck you. I'll see you around."

I grab my bag, and I'm about to walk out when we're both startled by Rose, who unbeknown to us has been standing there listening.

She starts to yell at him, unleashing every ounce of anger from deep within. "Dad, why are you blaming Lauren? This isn't Lauren's fault."

He turns to face her, his voice carrying a no-nonsense authority and finality. "Go to your room this instant. This is between me and Lauren."

"I will not," she yells back.

If I've learnt anything today, it's that this isn't my argument. He's made it perfectly clear he's happy to fuck me but that's all. As much as he relented and introduced me to Rose, I finally accept that there's no room for me in this part of his life. What did I think was going to happen? That we were going to play happy families? That I'd be helping with homework every night?

A solitary tear trickles down my cheek as my whole being aches from disappointment. There's nothing left for me to say. There's only one thing left for me to do, and that's walk out of the door, closing it behind me, closing it on my relationship with Mark and any hope I had of being a part of his life—of being wanted and cherished by the man I gave my heart to.

Mark

I faintly hear the door closing, but I'm too angry right now to fully comprehend that Lauren has walked out and that I should perhaps go after her. But I'm only a man, and I can only deal with one hormonal female at a time.

I turn to Rose, who is attempting to make a retreat. "Where do you think you're going? I haven't finished with you," I say sternly, and despite trying my best to try to not explode, there is a hint of anger thrown in. "You're not old enough to have sex, but for God's sake please tell me you used protection."

"Oh my God! I'm not having this conversation with you."

"I don't expect you to share everything with me. You have your friends and your mother for that particular topic. But I know what goes on in the mind of teenage boys. I was one myself. They tend not to think with their minds but with their dicks."

I realise I've been too crude when her eyes widen in surprise, but my anger doesn't subside as I continue my tirade. "And as your father, I'm going to make damn well sure that you make good choices; and having sex at fifteen is not a good choice. So what in God's name were you thinking."

She volleys her words at me. "I can't reason with you. You won't listen to anything I have to say. It feels like you're controlling my life. It's not fair; I'm going to be sixteen in a few weeks. It shouldn't be a big deal if I want to have a boyfriend. Why can't you trust me? I don't actually need your approval you know."

"I can't trust you because you've already proven your lack of judgment with this latest stunt."

She sighs in exasperation. "For your information, I have not had sex. But if I wanted to have sex, then it would be my decision since it's my body. I can go to the doctor and get birth control, and you wouldn't know anything about it."

I'm taking in her words. Relief washes over me knowing she hasn't had sex. I'm also feeling deeply proud of her determination to stick up for herself. Pleased to know that she's thought of birth control. Perhaps I am being too hard on her.

But the feeling is short lived when she metaphorically kicks me in the gut.

"You had sex with mum when she was seventeen. Who's to say you didn't take advantage of her; you were five years older. So you're a fine one to try and lecture me."

My temper is boiling up as I holler at her. "Go to your room right now, young lady." I raise my arm and point in the direction of her bedroom.

"Young lady? Oh my God! You're such a jerk."

"Don't you dare speak to me like that. I'm your father, and as such you will show me some respect."

"Why should I? You don't show me any. You never listen to anything I say. Why can't you ever see things from my point of view? And look how you've just treated Lauren. She didn't do anything wrong. She was trying to help. You're being a bully. You're acting like a juvenile. And here I am thinking that's my job. I'm supposed to be the immature teenager."

"I don't need Lauren's help. And you had no right going to her and dragging her in to family business."

"Business! Is that how you see me? Do you schedule meetings with mum to discuss me like you do with work? You've driven away the one person you've ever been with that I actually like. You're cold and heartless, and poor Lauren is better off without you. I hate you. I hate you."

She gives me a look of such absolute fury that in that moment I truly believe that she does hate me.

"You're grounded!"

"Oh please. What are you going to do, lock me in my room? Get a life, Dad." She spins around like a cyclone and storms off to her room, slamming the door behind her with such force that I swear I can feel the whole apartment block tremor.

"Fucking women." I pour myself a stiff drink and down it in one gulp, then replenish my glass. I recline on the sofa and close my eyes. I pinch the bridge of my nose to ease the pressure building up in my head. I take a couple of deep breaths and exhale.

Just when I think I've managed to calm myself down, Rose's words play on a loop in my mind—*You've driven away the one person... You're cold and heartless, and Lauren is better off without you.*

It's then that I realise the magnitude of what's just happened.

CHAPTER 21
Lauren

Despite Mark's harsh and cruel words, I'm determined to carry on with my life, to try to forget that he made me feel insignificant. I try to forget that for the first few nights I cried myself to sleep with his words ringing in my ears.

He never came after me. He hasn't called or messaged me. And yet I still make excuses for him. Is it stupidity or love? I think we'll go for stupid. Stupid for falling in love with a man who isn't capable of loving me back.

Neither have I heard from Rose, and I find myself hoping she's okay, that the situation with the boob pic has been dealt with effectively, and she can go back to being a carefree teenager.

So it's an understatement to say I'm excited as I arrive for my lunch date at a popular contemporary restaurant in Soho that serves classic British food. It's very understated; the furnishings are simple, reminiscent of a school canteen, making me almost feel like a teenager again. But it's the natural light beaming through the glass atrium that really sets the atmosphere.

I spot him as soon as I walk through the door. My jaw is

aching from the grin I can't seem to contain.

In my excitement, I don't wait for the hostess, I head straight for the table where he's seated. I've been excited ever since he called me two days ago to let me know he'd be back in London. We made immediate plans to meet today.

As soon as I reach his table, he looks up and an instant, easy smile spreads across his face. "Lauren. You look great."

He stands, walks around to my side of the table, gives me a big warm hug, kisses me on the cheek, then pulls out the chair for me.

"Hi, Pete." When I sit, I notice he's already ordered me a gin and tonic, and I immediately have a sip. "Thanks for pre-ordering my drink. It's been a bit of a shitty morning so far at work. Great choice of restaurant by the way. I guess you missed British food on your travels."

"Yeah, as much as I loved my stint working in Brazil, it's good to be home. Thought it about time I check up on everything and everyone. Plus I missed the rain. I missed you."

We're interrupted when the server approaches to take our order, but we get straight back into it as soon as he disappears.

"I missed you too. It's good to have you back in town, even if it's just a flying visit. How have you been? Tell me everything you've been up to. What are your plans? How long are you staying in London?"

There's a faint chuckle at my eagerness to hear all about his travels. "Okay, slow down. I'm here until the next job. Probably about a month, so I'd like us to spend as much quality time together as we can. We need to make up for lost time."

"I'd like that. Don't you ever get tired of travelling the globe taking photos?"

"You know me. Itchy feet. Can't stay put for too long."

While we catch up on what we've both been up to, time seems to fly by. It always does when I'm listening to tales of Pete's adventures.

Pete's last sentence trails off as he looks past me, one brow rises questioningly as his eyes dart back to me.

I feel the hairs on the back of my neck stand on end and goosebumps tingle over my skin, and I know without turning around who is standing behind me.

"Well, well, well. The first sign of trouble and you revert to default. Moving on to the next unsuspecting guy. Chasing the next score and your thirst for gratification, all without a backward glance."

I don't have time to say anything in response as I notice Pete's eyes darken as he spears a venomous look at Mark. Everything that happens next is in slow motion. He takes his napkin and wipes the corners of his mouth. He stands, walks around to place himself in front of Mark, and punches him on the jaw.

I'm shocked as I watch Mark's head ricochet off Pete's fist when it makes contact.

"Don't ever talk about my sister like that again."

Mark straightens his shoulders. He rubs the side of his jaw with his hand. His fingers lightly trace the corner of his mouth to see if there's any blood. There isn't. As bad as it looked, I don't think it was that hard. He raises his chin and looks at me with a cool stare.

Around us, all activity has ceased, and the restaurant is silent as everyone from the diners to the staff have stopped to watch this performance and how it plays out. Guess we won't we dining here again any time soon.

The hostess has called upon the manager to intervene, and I worry that we'll be asked to leave. I pre-empt him and quickly rise to my feet, propelled by the explosiveness of the situation, and yank Pete's arm. "Leave it. He's not worth it."

There's talk of police being called, but Mark puts a halt to that with a dismissive wave of his hand. I expect him to hurl a barrage of expletives or at least have some sort of retort, but he doesn't. He doesn't speak at all.

I try to avoid his stare, but his eyes capture mine. Even now, when I want to grab him by the scruff of the neck and strangle him, I'm finding it hard to fight my feelings for him, and it's as though he can read my thoughts, because his stare suddenly changes to one of amusement, and he offers a self-satisfied smirk. As if to let me know that he's acutely aware that I still have feelings for him.

I stand motionless as he turns on his heel. My eyes follow his tall frame as he casually strides towards his own table, as if nothing happened, as if the whole incident didn't even leave a chink in his armour.

When he reaches his table, my mouth is agape, and I feel my eyes widen in annoyance when I notice his lunch date is an attractive blonde, in her early-late thirties I'd guess. Talk about hypocritical.

I prise my eyes away, no sense in torturing myself, and I sit back down opposite Pete. We sit silently for a few seconds before he speaks, but the ferocity of his voice and his words bely the unruffled exterior he attempts to portray but fails.

Pete's anger is evident even before he utters a word, as he glares at me, eyes ablaze with fury. "Who the fuck is that?"

"Just some guy I was seeing for a while."

"Just some guy? Don't ever put up with anyone talking about you, or to you, like that, do you hear me?"

"Yes, I hear you. Loud and clear. The whole restaurant can hear you. But he's not like that, not really. I think he was taken by surprise seeing me, that's all."

"Jesus Christ, Lauren, stop making excuses for him. He's a grown-arsed man. He should be able to control himself. This is why you keep meeting losers. Don't stand for any shit."

Amongst all the emotions I've been feeling over the last few weeks, even though I know my brother is just looking out for me, it feels like I'm being scolded.

"I know you mean well. I know you feel it's your duty, but I could really do without a lecture right now." I quickly glance over my shoulder to where Mark is seated, but I'm caught out by Pete.

As he allows his anger to simmer, his voice softens at the sight of my quivering lip. "I guess you really like this one. Want to tell me about it?"

I sigh as I sit back. "He has a daughter, and she comes first. It's as simple as that."

"He's divorced?"

"Never married. But apparently it's all very amicable. They share custody. I wasn't around long enough to find out much else. He completely lost it when his daughter came to me for help with boy trouble, and I stupidly thought I was doing the right thing in supporting her. He completely freaked out about it. So I walked out. That was a couple of weeks ago. I haven't seen or had any contact with him until today."

He seems pensive as his brows draw together. The anger seems to have completely subsided, and he offers me a small smile. "I suppose I can understand where he's coming from with regard to protecting his daughter. When Dad passed away, I felt it was my responsibility to take care of you, protect you, and that included from lecherous boys. All I'm going to say is, you deserve better than to be spoken to like that."

"Hang on a minute, does this explain why no one would ask me out at school? Do you know how much I cried because all my friends had boyfriends except for me? Thanks a lot, big brother."

He shifts uncomfortably in his chair and then we both burst out laughing.

Mark

When I get to my table Shelby's brows are drawn together disapprovingly; her mouth is tight and grim. She takes a sip of her wine, giving me a few seconds of respite before she says anything.

"Well, that performance is not what I anticipated when you invited me to lunch."

I pull out my chair and sit. The pain in my jaw has me speaking through gritted teeth. "I don't want to talk about it." She's barely able to contain her amusement as her lips tremble with the need to laugh at my predicament. "I'm glad you find this funny."

"Oh please. I know you better than you know yourself. And knowing you as well as I do, I'm in no doubt that you thoroughly deserved what you got. I take it that's Lauren I've been hearing so much about from Rose?"

"I need a drink. Do you want another." She shakes her head, and I motion for the server and order a scotch.

"Let's order so we can discuss Rose's birthday. After that you can fill me in on everything Rose has left out about Lauren."

It seems that Rose has been cleverly working on persuading her mother that Lauren's concept of a rooftop venue is a good one. And since it appears that I'm outnumbered, I'm in no mood to argue. If only I could have realised that two weeks ago, then perhaps I wouldn't have driven Lauren away.

I'm jolted back to the here and now by Shelby's forthright question. "Now, about this other little problem. How do you want to handle it? Are we going to go to the school or direct to the parents?"

"Apparently, I'm incapable of making the right decisions at the moment, so I'll follow your lead. What do you think we should do?"

"Go to the parents. Hopefully, he hasn't circulated it, and we can contain it. Going to the school will have it out there and the talk of the school gossip before you know it. I'm pretty friendly with Melissa Ashbrook, so I'll call her and arrange a meeting."

"Yeah, you're probably right. What I'm more concerned about is why Rose felt she couldn't come to either of us. I understand that she didn't want to tell me, but she should have been able to come to you. Are we that strict that she's too afraid to come to either of us when she has a problem?"

"Mark, don't beat yourself up about it. Oops, sorry, someone's already done that for you."

I give her a sour grin. "Very funny. Let's just stick to the topic at hand shall we."

There's a slight pause, allowing me to take another sip of my drink before she speaks calmly but matter-of-factly.

"She's a teenager. They're supposed to be angsty and

rebellious. Everything and anything we do as parents will be deemed as interfering. Teenagers want to carve out their identity independent of their parents. It's all perfectly normal. All part and parcel of growing up. Perhaps you should try and remember your teenage years once in a while."

"That's exactly why I do worry. I remember very clearly you as a seventeen-year-old vixen. You seemed to enjoy all of the male attention. In fact, I'd go so far as to say you craved it."

"Yes, I was quite flirtatious and full of myself. And once I'd set my sights on you, there was no stopping me." She leans in, rests her forearms on the table, one hand covering mine. The intensity of her lowered voice only serves to emphasise its sultriness; something that years ago, when I was a strapping twenty-two-year-old, was all it took to get me into bed. Lauren was right about one thing —I'm an easy fuck. "The sex was pretty amazing. You have to admit, we were good together."

Never as good as it was with Lauren. "That was then. This is now. But I've no regrets. We wouldn't have Rose if we hadn't hooked-up."

"I'm not sure I've ever said it, but thanks for sticking by me when everyone else around me tried to ram their thoughts and opinions of what was best for me down my throat. Thank you for being part of her life, for being my best friend."

I take her hand and bring it to my lips and place a light kiss on the back of her hand. "I should thank you for giving me Rose. Even if she is a stubborn, know-it-all, little madam, I wouldn't have it any other way."

"I guess she gets that from me. And since I'm a know-it-all, why don't you fill me in on what I don't know. Tell me

more about Lauren."
 "Where do I begin."

CHAPTER 22

Mark

I arrive at my mother's house in north London for our weekly dinner to find her and Rose in the kitchen. The place is a complete mess: pots, bowls, and utensils scattered everywhere. A dusting of flour all over the island worktop.

"What do we have here?" I kiss my mother on the cheek and ruffle Rose's hair affectionately, but annoyingly for her. I shake off my suit jacket and throw it idly on one of the stools.

"We're making dumplings for the casserole."

"And is there a specific reason why you're going all out for a weekday meal?"

"Yes, I've invited a dinner guest," Rose says.

My eyes narrow, and I shoot my mother a sceptical glance.

"Oh, don't look at me like that. It's about time you started to date properly. You remember the Crosby's, don't you? Well, Elizabeth just moved back to London. I remember the two of you being as thick as thieves when you were children. It would be lovely to see her again, wouldn't it?"

I loosen my tie. "Mother, we had this discussion a few days ago, and I told you then that I don't have any interest in Elizabeth Crosby. You need to stop with the matchmaking. It didn't work when I was younger. It's not going to work now."

"You can't blame a mother for wanting to see her children happily settled. You know I love and adore Shelby, and I think it's admirable how the two of you have managed to stay close and navigate bringing up Rose, but I don't want you to be on your own. Shelby has someone wonderful. I just want the same for you. I worry about you, that's all. You seem so closed off."

This is typical of my mother. Trying to coax me into revealing information. Even though I know what she's doing, I'm never able to keep anything from her for too long. "I'm sure Rose must have mentioned that I've met someone."

There's a flash of movement as their eyes dart to each other, and they give each other a conspiratorial look.

Rose continues to roll dumplings in her palms, looking guilty as sin, and my mother continues to lecture.

"From what I hear, that's over with."

"Christ, Mother, do I look eighteen years old? I really don't need the pep talk. And as it happens, I'm working on it not being over. I just haven't come up with how."

"So, you'd like to rekindle things with this young lady? Am I permitted to know a little about her?"

I look in Rose's direction just as she looks up at me, her smirk letting me know how much she's enjoying seeing me get the third degree.

"Somehow I think you already know everything there is to know."

"Humour me, dear."

I sigh, consoling myself with my memories, able to picture every detail of her face, recalling the smouldering passion between us at each touch. "Her name is Lauren."

"You say her name with such affection. Why don't you tell me more about her. What makes her different from all the others? What makes her so special?"

"So many things. I can give you a whole list of her attributes." My mind is momentarily lost in thought as I'm flooded with memories until Rose interrupts, her voice casually urging me to reveal more.

"Go on then, Dad."

I clear my throat. For a miniscule of a second, I feel uncomfortable to be discussing this with my mother and daughter. But then the thought of Lauren and an opportunity to talk about her brightens my mood, and my uneasiness is left behind.

"She's beautiful. But it's not just her physical beauty. She's beautiful inside too. She's affectionate and gentle." I shake my head to rid visions of how gentle she is when she has my dick in her hand.

"She's smart. Independent. She makes me laugh at the most ridiculous things. The way her face lights up when she's laughing makes me fall a little more in love with her each time. She's also assertive. She gives as good as she gets. But as you've no doubt heard, I screwed things up."

"Dad, Lauren loves you."

"You were there. I said some shitty stuff to her. In fact I'd say it was pretty unforgivable."

"Have you sent her some flowers to say sorry? That always works."

"I think things have gone beyond that. I don't think sorry is going to cut it. I bumped into her a few days ago when I met your mother for lunch, and I said some not very complimentary things to her then too. And just to make sure I did a good job I practically called her a slut in public."

"Mark Taylor, enough of that language in front of your daughter."

"I'm sure Rose has heard worse." We exchange a smirk. Perhaps I am becoming a little more relaxed, less strict. When her mother and I sat down with her and had a long chat about everything, I made a deal with Rose that I would do my best not to be a stick in the mud, an old fart. "Dad, you're not even forty yet. Even Adam is way cooler than you" is how she undiplomatically put it.

Rose finally shows her anger. She raises her voice and throws the dumpling on to the island. "Jesus, Dad. How bloody hard is it to say you're sorry?"

Raised eyebrows, coupled with a stern look, indicate my mother's displeasure at Rose's outburst. "Language, young lady."

They exchange a polite, simultaneous smile. "Sorry, Gran."

"Anyway, I haven't invited Elizabeth, she wasn't free this evening. I'm just here to help with the food, then I'll be on my way. So why don't you go and freshen up while we finish up here."

"Great, that's all I need right now, a blind date. Did we have to do it here, in my personal space? Why couldn't it just be drinks at a bar? How am I supposed to get rid of her?" I pull my tie over my head as I walk away, muttering under my breath at the absurdity of a grown-arsed man being bullied into a date by his mother and fifteen-year-old daughter.

I hear my mother calling out after me. "All I think about is your happiness. And you'll thank me in years to come for pushing you a little."

I take a shower and change into jeans and a T-shirt from the clothes I keep here. If they think I'm going to make any effort to impress, they're sorely mistaken. I've resigned myself to the fact that I've lost Lauren. If I can't have her, then I really don't want anyone.

I'll go back to what I do best—meaningless sex. Because clearly I've no idea how to hold on to the one woman I've ever loved.

Memories are a strange phenomenon. I always seem to remember the same things, when there are so many other things, like how her laughter rings in my ears. The curves of her body that fit snuggly to mine. She's perfect for me in every way. Images of us together play on my mind, constantly taunting me with what I've lost.

By the time I've resurfaced to the living room, mother is putting her jacket on. She gives me a dissatisfied glance at my casual look and tut-tuts when she notices I'm barefoot.

I do the gentlemanly thing and walk her to the door. As I open it for her, she turns to me. "Rose has gone to a lot of effort for you." She reaches out and gently and lovingly pats my cheek like she used to when I was a kid, and then she says with her ordered voice of authority, "Don't fuck this up."

Too startled to say anything, I close the door and walk to the living room.

I look on disapprovingly as Rose is putting the final touches to the table. Candles, the best silver, crystal wine glasses.

"This is all rather over the top, don't you think?"

"Dad, you need to go all out to impress if you want to win the woman."

"Who said I want to impress, let alone win the woman. I just want tonight to be over with. So feel free to interrupt us after an hour has passed."

The buzzer goes startling us both. "Fuck."

"Dad, stop swearing. Promise you'll be on your best behaviour."

I'm walking to the door to press the entry button as I look back over my shoulder at Rose. "I'm not promising anything since I've been bulldozed into this. If she doesn't like it, she can lump it."

But when I open the door my mouth is agape, and for once in my life, I'm left utterly and completely speechless. Standing before me is the most beautiful woman I've ever seen.

My gaze takes hold of her, searching her body up and down as if she's just appeared from a dream.

Luscious auburn hair cascading past her shoulders. Hazel eyes alight with a golden glow and sweeping lashes. Full pink lips that I instantly want to devour with my own.

Tall and graceful with a body to die for, a body I want to lie down with and cover with my own. A body sheathed in tight-fitting skinny jeans, an oversized T-shirt that's falling off one shoulder revealing soft ivory skin that's calling to me, begging me to drop my lips on that creamy flesh and kiss my way from her shoulder to her neck to behind her ear. As my eyes slowly roam over her body from head to toe, don't think I haven't noticed the fuck-me heels with her red-painted toenails peeking out.

When my eyes move upward to meet hers, they're sparkling, looking back at me seductively, drawing me in. I wonder if she can tell how much I want her right now. How desperate I am to have her, be inside her, make mad passionate love to her.

She seems nervous as she runs a hand over her hair and tucks a lock behind her ear. I notice how she's clutching her bag tightly in the other hand.

I swallow the lump in my throat that's preventing me from speaking.

"Hi. Come in."

I step aside to allow her to pass and close the door behind her. I point in the direction of the living room, and my eyes follow her, fixated on how her hips sway, how perfect her arse looks in her tight-fitting jeans, making me want to grab her from behind, but I exercise restraint. I drink in the sensuality of her figure as she sashays into the living room with me trailing behind like a dog on heat. Practically salivating at the thought of getting my leg over that body.

Why the fuck am I nervous? In fact, my nervousness almost has me forget my manners until I'm the one in desperate need of a drink to calm me down.

"Would you like a drink?"

"Thanks, red wine would be nice if you have it." She follows me farther into the living room, puts her bag on the sofa, just as Rose comes out of the kitchen.

"Lauren," she squeals. "You came!" She rushes over and gives Lauren the biggest, tightest hug imaginable, making my heart swell.

"Of course I came, silly. Why wouldn't I?" She looks over at me before adding, "I was expecting this to be a girls' night. I can leave if you prefer."

"No. Dad, tell her not to leave."

I hand Lauren her wine and pour myself a scotch. "Who am I to argue with a teenager." In that moment, an affectionate smile passes between us, giving me hope that maybe I can somehow salvage this relationship.

"The casserole should be ready in about half an hour. I've made the salad; all you have to do is dish it up and eat. Cheesecake is in the fridge." She proceeds to grab her rucksack and slings it over one shoulder.

"And where do you think you're going?"

"I'm staying at Mum's tonight. It's all arranged. And Gran won't be back for ages. She's playing bridge with Mrs Stanley next door. I'll see you tomorrow. You kids have fun," she says, laughing as she walks out the door.

I turn my attention to Lauren and gesture to the sofa. "Shall we sit down?"

She moves to join me on the sofa. "I'm sorry, I really had no idea. She told me you were in Brussels for work. I would never have come if I'd known."

"Why not?" I ask, trying to hide my disappointment.

"Why not what?"

"Why wouldn't you have come?"

There's a one shoulder shrug. "I think you've made it clear where things stand between us."

"Yeah, about that." I place my glass down on the table and move closer to her, my thigh lightly touching hers, as I bump her shoulder with mine. I take her glass and place it beside mine. "I know I haven't handled things very well."

Her hands are clasped together tightly, giving me the impression that she's trying to control her emotions as much as I am. "Yes, you could say you've been a bit of a bastard."

"I guess I deserve that. In my defence, I was afraid. I didn't know what to do, how to handle things, let alone even admit to myself how I feel about you. My priority has always been Rose. I've been doing it for so long, it's ingrained in me. I don't know how to let go a little, even if I want to."

"I guess I should take some of the blame. Maybe I could have been a little less selfish and a little more understanding."

"No, don't you dare take any responsibility for this. It's all on me."

I notice the moisture glistening in her eyes and decide to change the topic of conversation. I'm sure making her cry is not part of the plan.

"Let's eat."

Lauren

Once we finish dinner, we move back to the living room. I sink into the sofa, kick my shoes off, and draw my legs up underneath my body. I take a sip of my wine that has been replenished at least twice since I got here, which probably accounts for my feeling so comfortable and relaxed.

"That was really lovely. I take it you had no hand in the food preparation."

Mark sits at the other end of the sofa. "Nope. That would be Rose and my mother. I'll readily admit that cooking is not one of my strong points. Toast, eggs, cereal, I can manage."

I smile at his self-deprecation. "How you've survived I'll never know. But I wouldn't worry about it, you have other skills that more than make up for it."

He moves closer and reaches up to smooth my hair with his hand. The depth of his brown eyes irresistible as they hold mine. Glowing with appreciation, filled with longing.

"I miss you, Lauren. I want to be able to wake up beside you, lean across and kiss you, before leaping out of bed to make you breakfast. You're the one I've always wished for."

I let out a breath. Never have I ever wanted someone so much. Never have I loved someone so much. But I've learnt that I need to live in the real world, not some hope of a happy ever after fairy tale scenario. I'll leave that to Hollywood.

"I miss you too. But you know what, I love myself more. I don't deserve a man who's preoccupied. I won't be second place or second choice. I want someone to choose me for once. I want to be someone's first choice. That's what I deserve. I've worked hard to get where I am. I may not be at the top of my profession, but I consider myself successful. I have my own place. I pay my own bills. I don't need a man to improve my social standing. I'm not a Susanna. All I want is love. Someone to love me unconditionally. Is that too much to ask?"

"No it's not. I sure as hell don't deserve you, and yes, you deserve better than me. But I've realised that I don't have to choose. It's not a question of you or Rose. I've accepted that I can still be a decent father and have a romantic relationship. I don't know, maybe it's because it's you that it just seems right. And please don't forget the most important thing in all of this."

"And what's that?"

"I love you. I know you love me back. Don't try and deny it."

"You say the words *I love you* as if they will magically solve everything." I look away, my eyes focusing on anything but him, so I won't be distracted by his velvety brown eyes as they glow with tenderness and his breathy words that I waited so long to hear.

"All I'm asking is that you don't close the door on us."

As he looks at me hopefully, it feels as though the pain I feel is going to perforate my heart as I answer him. "How can I. You never even had it open for me."

I focus on being able to say my next words, knowing they're harsh, knowing they hurt me as much as they may hurt him. But I have to be strong. I need to do this so that I can grow whole again, move on.

"Maybe it's too little too late."

CHAPTER 23
Mark

As the weeks roll by, I find myself staring at my phone. I'm constantly willing it to ring or ping with a text. But no amount of psyche is going to work. Her words were final. There's a constant recollection echoing in my mind as her words torture me— it's too little too late. Now all I have are the memories I'm left with, burning an imprint on my mind.

I torture myself at the thought of there being no shortage of men to keep her company. There's certainly no shortage of women for me to hook up with, but I have absolutely no interest in any other woman.

So it's with some relief at the prospect of being able to take my mind off things that I accept an invitation to dinner at Adam and Jules's home.

"Why do I feel like I've been ambushed?"

We're sitting in the kitchen as Jules places a bowl of spaghetti with meat balls in tomato sauce in front of me. "We're not bulldozing you or ambushing you."

"Hey, less of the we, this was all your idea," says Adam.

She narrows her eyes at him and then turns to me with a smile plastered across her face. The same smile that more than likely had Adam hook, line, and sinker from the very first moment he saw her.

She sits down and watches me tuck into my food. And call me cynical, but it's not until I have a mouth full of food and I'm unable to speak that she decides this is the moment to give me what feels like a lecture.

"You have to be the one to reach out. You need to let her know how you feel, what you want. You need to prove to her you want her, let her know you're ready, and willing to let her in. Not because the sex is great, but because you love her."

I swallow with a gulp and wipe my lips with my napkin. "Hang on a second. Who said anything about reaching out? I already tried that, and she shot me down. And why are you putting this all on me? She hasn't made any effort to contact me. This works both ways."

"Oh my God. You, Mark Taylor, are almost as stubborn as my husband. You told her she was interfering. You told her in no uncertain terms that Rose would always come first. That you had no time for her. You practically told her you just wanted to screw her when it suits you. What do you expect her to do?"

I find myself on the defensive. "I said no such thing."

"You may not have said those exact words, but what you said and how you said it made her interpret it that way. And don't think I don't know what happened when you saw her having lunch with her brother. That was nasty and spiteful. And quite frankly, I'm disappointed in you."

I glance over at Adam as he sits twirling spaghetti around his fork. "Hey, man, care to help me out here?"

He smirks. Enjoying seeing me being put on the spot by Jules. "Nope."

"For your information, I tried. Rose blindsided me and invited her to my mother's house for dinner. I told her exactly how I feel, and she threw it back in face."

"You see, this is exactly what I'm talking about. It's all about *you*. You told her how *you* feel. She threw it back in *your* face. What about Lauren and how she's feeling?"

"She made her feelings pretty clear."

"So you're giving up, is that it?"

I place my fork down and push my plate forward. "For fuck's sake, what do you expect me to do?"

Adam glares at me with burning, reproachful eyes. "What you need to do is calm down."

No doubt it's our friendship that's prevented him for taking a swing at me for speaking to Jules in that way. I rake a hand through my hair. "I'm really sorry, Jules. Please forgive me. But can we stop talking about Lauren. I'm trying my best to forget."

Adam shakes his head. "As someone who's been there and tried that, good luck. You're going to need it."

"Fuck off."

"Guys, stop it. We're supposed to be brainstorming, coming up with a plan. What you need to do is show her what she means to you."

"Yeah, okay. Whatever you say, Jules."

"What Jules is trying to tell you is that you need to be a little more… proactive. Fight for what you want."

What is it I want? As for what I would want in a potential partner, the thought has never crossed my mind. Because I've never been looking for a lifelong partner. I've never been in the market for a stepmother for my daughter. My one and only concern has always been Rose and what's best for her. That's why I never introduce her to the women I fuck. On the rare occasion that she did meet two of the women with whom I engaged in sexual gratification, she'd taken an instant dislike to them. But for a reason that I'm unable to fathom, she seems to like Lauren. Perhaps I shouldn't be so surprised. Anyone in their right mind would love Lauren. She's had an effect on me that I would never have imagined possible.

Adam is one of my best friends and having watched him take that step to his happily ever after, somewhere in the back of my mind I would occasionally wonder if I'd ever meet a woman who would completely floor me—bowl me over in the way that Jules somehow managed to completely captivate Adam.

Then Lauren appeared, the answer to all my prayers that I didn't even know I'd made. From the moment I laid eyes on her, she took my breath away, so much so that I had to have her beneath me, on top of me, every which way possible. I should have known from our first night together and the sense of fulfilment that one night of being with her gave me. She had me fantasizing for more. I wanted to feel the ecstasy deeper. I wanted to experience it repeatedly. My heart took a perilous leap that night without my even realising.

And now I'm constantly consumed with thoughts of Lauren. Even work doesn't manage to distract me. I go over and over everything.

I should have stopped things before they went too far, before I broke her heart. I realise that now. Of all the mistakes I've made, that's the biggest.

CHAPTER 24

Lauren

I agreed to dinner at her grandmother's because for some reason I'm bearing some of the responsibility for what happened. I felt guilty for the fact that Rose had to witness our heated argument and breakup. I wanted to apologise. I wanted her to know none of this is her fault. The last thing I was expecting was for her to set me up. Although I have to say, there's something endearing in the fact that Rose is trying her utmost to get Mark and me back together.

I'm not entirely sure what's brought me here today. I'm undecided whether it's still a little guilt or if it's plain old-fashioned curiosity. I will admit to being surprised that she called me, since the dinner with Mark that she lovingly prepared with her grandmother's help didn't quite net the result she was hoping for.

We're meeting during my lunch break at an ice cream parlour near my work, as if I haven't already devoured endless tubs of Ben and Jerry's in an attempt to console myself and stave off my tears at the sense of loss I feel.

We're both tucking into a classic Knickerbocker Glory—neither one of us wanting to start the conversation we both know we're here for.

As the grown up, I suppose it's on me to get the ball rolling. "How's your dad?"

"He's being a grump."

"What about your situation with Dan?"

She continues scooping out ice cream on to her spoon while she talks. "It's been dealt with. My mum called his mum, and they arranged a meeting of the parents. Blah blah blah."

"Well, I'm really glad to hear that. I hope they gave him a good talking-to."

"He actually apologised to me the next day. Asked to walk home with me from school and everything."

"That sounds like a good outcome. So you're friends now?"

She looks up at me, her eyes gleaming, a satisfied smile brightening her face. "Actually, he's asked me to go on a date."

"So you've forgiven him?"

"Yeah, everyone makes mistakes, don't they?"

I pretend not to notice her subtle reference to my situation with Mark. "Wow! That's a great outcome. And can I say it's very mature of you to forgive him. When are you going on this date?"

"Next week. We're going for pizza. But Dad doesn't know yet. I have to break it to him gently. I'm just waiting for the right time."

"Hmm, we all know how overprotective your dad can be." I smile at her, my comment not meant to be anything but a statement of fact.

As she looks at me, there's a hint of sorrow in her eyes. "I'm so sorry, Lauren."

"Hey, what have you got to be sorry about?"

"Dad and his reaction. It's all my fault, and now you're not together anymore."

I feel a surge of protectiveness for Rose. She's taking the weight of mine and Mark's situation on her shoulders. I do my best to reassure her that nothing about this is her fault.

"I think you're giving yourself too much credit. Your dad is old enough to take responsibility for his actions."

"Do you miss him?"

That's the million-dollar question, and I'm slightly taken aback that she's actually asked it. It's the question I've been trying not to ask myself. It's something I've been trying to convince myself I'm not feeling.

"I'm not sure I should be discussing this with you, Rose. But yes, of course I miss him."

Her face brightens. "He misses you too."

It's hard not to be curious how she's come to this conclusion. "Really. And how would you know that?"

"I already told you. He's turned into a grump. He comes home and mopes around. He sits on the sofa flicking aimlessly through the TV channels. Even Adam has been over to try to coax him from his depression. He's managed to persuade him to go play squash a few times. But other than that, he's on autopilot. He gets up in the morning and goes to work, then comes home. If it wasn't for Gran coming over to cook, we'd starve. Every day is the same, like *Groundhog Day*. And he's drinking more than usual too."

I'm struggling to picture Mark down in the dumps. I'm sure there are plenty of women available to help him take his mind of things—help him relax, massage his ego and anything else he wants.

"Can't you forgive him, like I've forgiven Dan, and give

him another chance?"

"This is where the problem lies. You shouldn't be sitting here pleading his case. He's a lawyer for crying out loud. It should be him sitting opposite me. He had plenty to say at your grandmother's, but they're just words. They don't mean anything. He's always been good at saying exactly what you would want to hear. Actions speak louder than words. He should be the one doing everything he can to make amends. But he hasn't. I'm afraid you have to face the fact that he doesn't want to."

"No, he does. I know he does."

"Has he told you that?"

"No, but I can tell. Maybe it's because he doesn't know how. He's never had to before."

"Well, he can Google it." Sarcasm has always been my strong point.

"Please, Lauren, would you just come and see him?"

"I know what I'm saying sounds harsh, Rose, but I think you need to let things go. I know it's hard, believe me. The most important thing is that your dad loves you more than anything. It took me a while, but I've realised it's not just me. Any woman that comes into his life is inconsequential.

"Maybe one day he'll meet the woman of his dreams. A woman he won't be able to let go, and if he loves her, I'm certain you will too."

"But he loves you, I know he does. I've never ever seen him like this, ever."

"Let's agree to disagree and change to subject. How are things with school?"

Her shoulders slump. "Yeah, they're fine." She puts the final scoop of ice cream in her mouth.

"And how are the plans going for your sixteenth birthday party?"

"Mum's been busy organising. Dad is helping too. We went to view a rooftop venue like you suggested. It's pretty cool."

"Well that's good, isn't it?"

"I suppose."

"I'm sure it's going to be fun. You have so much to look forward to, Rose. Don't let what's happened between your dad and me spoil this time for you. And don't be affected by whoever comes next. Promise me you'll concentrate on yourself. Work hard to achieve the grades you need to get into university."

She looks at me in sudden realisation, her eyes clouded with tears. "Is this your way of saying goodbye?"

I know what I have to do. I have to be cruel to be kind. "I'm not sure us meeting on a regular basis is a good idea for either of us. As harsh as it sounds, I need to get on with my life without a constant reminder." She nods as the tears in her eyes threaten to trickle down her cheeks. I reach across the table and place my hand over hers.

"Don't be sad. I'm so grateful that we met. You've reminded me of my younger self. Full of energy, ready to fight the world. Don't lose that. Stay true to yourself and forge your path, one that makes you happy. Your dad will want nothing less for you—I want nothing less for you."

I glance at my watch. It's gone two o'clock. My lunch hour is over. "I'm afraid I have to get back to work."

I grab my bag and stand. As I look at Rose, she's glancing down, as if she's trying to think of what to say or what her next move should be. "Are you okay?"

She nods. My heart bleeding for her. But I know I've done the right thing. It won't do either of us any good in the long run to cling on. "Come on, let's walk out together."

She grabs her rucksack, and we head out. As we stand on the pavement, it's as though she doesn't want to leave. She doesn't want to say goodbye.

It's instinct that makes me embrace her. I wrap my arms around her and hug her tight. "You're going to be just fine. I know it."

And just when I thought my heart couldn't ache any more than it already does, she says the words that I will forever cherish and hold close to my heart. "I love you, Lauren."

CHAPTER 25
Mark

One minute you're just plodding along living life to what you think is the fullest, but in fact it's just plain mundane. Then the next minute you fall in love, and everything feels different.

I close my laptop and stand up to look out of my office window at the London skyline. I watch as the sun slowly disappears and daylight fades. Even nature is reminding me of all things Lauren.

She appeared like a ray of sunshine, and I created a shit storm that ultimately resulted in driving her away from me.

As I look down to the street, there are so many bodies rushing to who knows where. I wonder if Lauren is amongst them. I wonder where she is now. What she's doing now. Who she's with now.

I berate myself for treating her the way I did. For hurting her. Even if I take Adam and Jules's advice, would she listen to me, could she ever forgive me?

I throw myself into work. On the days Rose stays with her mother, my workload is such that I will typically work until at least nine o'clock at night. I certainly would never leave the office earlier than eight o'clock.

When Rose is with me, I do everything in my power to be home by six thirty so we can sit down together and have dinner. Discuss how her day went. Help with schoolwork.

I've worked my butt off to make things up to Rose. My guilt has even convinced me, with a little prodding from Rose, to extend her curfew time by half an hour to ten o'clock.

But I've come to the realisation that I'm not staying at work late because I need to meet deadlines. I'm doing it because when Rose isn't staying with me, I've no reason to go home. I've no one to go home to. My mind starts imagining what it would be like to leave the office and be excited to get home. What would it be like if Lauren were there waiting for me? I picture pouring myself a stiff drink after a hard day at the office. I'd relax on my plush sofa with the woman of my dreams snuggled up in my arms. What would it feel like to go home to my adoring wife? Well, there's something I never thought I'd ever contemplate. But all of those things now feel beyond my reach. Because I've somehow managed to not only crush her dreams but mine too. Yeah, you could say I've well and truly fucked up.

If only I'd just gone with how I was feeling from the outset instead of denying the reality, then I wouldn't be a sad, pathetic specimen of a man pining for something that there's no longer any hope in hell of acquiring.

Fuck my life.

I grab my sports bag and head out to meet Adam.

I'm half an hour late, and by the time I get to the squash court and change, Adam has already worked up a sweat practicing solo.

"About fucking time. What kept you?"

I tap my racket to the palm of my hand. "Work. You know how it is."

"Nope. I don't have that problem anymore. I decided when I married Jules to spend less time at the office. And you know what? It wasn't a hard decision to make."

"Yeah, well, we all know you went soft when you met Jules."

"One of these days, Mark Taylor, you're going to be where I am. Tell me, how is the lovely Lauren?"

He grins at me, and I'm not quite sure if he's mocking me since he knows full well the ins and outs of our situation.

"Something tells me Jules has kept you in the picture."

"Your name is mentioned every now and then, along with a barrage of expletives, and then she goes quiet. I'm not stupid enough to ask her what's going on. I just assume that since her little talk with you, nothing has changed."

He doesn't waste any more time with idle chat as he whacks the ball to the wall commencing our game. I hit it back before the second bounce.

We rally for forty minutes, neither of us letting up—Adam from sheer competitiveness, and me from my frustrations. Believe it or not, I find that pounding the ball, leaping, diving, stretching for the ball helps to relax my mind. Every thought is geared towards hitting the ball.

Adam is a worthy opponent. Our fitness levels are on par. While I make use of the weights at my home gym, I also like to increase my strength and fitness playing squash.

This is where I'm in my element. This is where I have complete control. Sports and work. And until recently I thought I had the parenting thing figured out. But when it comes to Lauren, I'm completely stumped.

After we've showered and changed, we walk out to the car park together and stop when we get to my car.

"You never answered my question."

"Which question would that be?"

"How are things going with Lauren? Made any headway?"

"Has Jules asked you to grill me? Or is this your impression of being a concerned friend?"

"Both."

"If you must know, nothing has changed. I've completely fucked the whole thing up. And yes, I did actually listen to what Jules said, but I can't see any way of coming back from it. Maybe I should have listened to you in the first place and stayed well away from her."

"Seems like you need cheering up. Why don't you join Jules and me for dinner tomorrow evening at the apartment? Once the baby arrives, we won't be entertaining for a while."

"Twice in one week? I'm not sure I'm up to being on the end of your wife's wrath again."

"She only does it because she loves you, both of you."

"As long as you ask Jules not to give me another dressing down."

"I can't promise anything. You know Jules. But she wants to make it up to you."

"Yeah, and you wouldn't have her any other way, right?"

He slaps me on the back. "Exactly, my friend."

Since Rose it at her mother's this entire week, organising her party, and rather than be at home alone, sulking, I decide to take Adam up on his offer. "What time would

you like me to grace you with my presence?"
　"Seven. I'm cooking, so don't be late."

Lauren

It's almost five thirty when Rachel comes by my desk. "Hey, Lauren." I look up from my screen to see her smiling face. "I'm leaving, but I'll see you at seven o'clock at Jules and Adam's."

There's a moment of silence as I feel my brows draw together while I try to make sense of what she's said.

Recognising my confusion she shakes her head. "Honestly, it's not my job to keep your social diary. The dinner party at Jules and Adam's place. Her pre-birth dinner? Don't tell me you've forgotten?"

"No, of course I haven't." *I just thought it was tomorrow evening.* "I have a gift and everything."

"Good. Tom is looking forward to seeing Pete and catching up. We'll see you there."

CHAPTER 26
Lauren

It's just a casual gathering with friends she said. It'll be fun she said.

Adam opens the door wearing a wide grin. "Hey, Lauren, glad you could make it." He gives me a welcoming kiss on the cheek and shakes Pete's hand, and I give him the gift bag as we enter. I can hear the sound of laughter and chatter, Rachel and Jules's distinct voices squealing excitedly.

Pete and I head to the living room to join them while Adam does the honours and gets us a drink.

They interrupt their conversation to greet us and then get right back into it. The topic of conversation amongst these cultured and intelligent people isn't world politics or saving the environment. Believe or not, the discussion under heavy debate is pizza toppings.

"Rachel always orders a margarita, then proceeds to eat half of my pepperoni," says Tom.

"Because I like pepperoni."

"Then why don't you just order your own, or better still, order a large one to share."

"But we share it anyway."

There's a twinkle of humour in his eyes as he looks at us and jokingly says, "Guess I'm not going to win on this one."

As their eyes meet, hers are full of pure adoration while his are overflowing with tenderness. And when he leans in and kisses her forehead, I can't help the joy overspilling inside of me at the sheer contentment Jules and Rachel have found with their partners.

The downside to being privy to such happiness is that it brings home the fact that I want that too. I'd hoped to have that with Andrew—he was a perfect match for me on paper. I liked him a lot. I could have fallen completely and utterly in love with him, but he proved to be a douchebag of epic proportions. And Mark Taylor, the man I'm actually hopelessly and madly in love with has decided that I'm not even worth the time and effort. After our unexpected dinner date at his mother's house, I expected him to up the ante—use everything in his arsenal—bring out the big guns—pull out all the stops to win me back. But I've had no communication from him. Complete silence for three whole weeks. My heart breaks when I think of poor Rose trying her damnedest to bring us back together. How ironic, the teen advising the grownups.

But seeing my friends blissfully happy also serves to reinforce the fact that it is achievable, and that's enough to give me hope for my future.

"What about crust? Thin or deep?" asks Pete. The unanimous verdict is definitely for thin crust.

The chatter continues as we move towards the dining table, which is set up in an area of the living room that is sectioned off by one of the large sofas. It's beautifully laid with the white and blue dining set and silver cutlery that I helped Jules pick out for her wedding gift list. There are three cream pillar candles in glass holders, placed down the centre and two small vases of pink carnations placed between them. It's not too overstated. It's perfect for a casual dinner party.

Then I notice the place settings more closely. "Jules, you have an odd number of place settings. Who else is coming?"

Her forehead creases as she shifts uncomfortably on the spot. Unable to look me directly in the eye, she stares down at the floor. She bites her bottom lip as she finally lifts her head to look at me.

She lowers her voice, almost hesitant to even speak. "Please don't be angry. Adam invited Mark, and we couldn't uninvite him. That would have been rude. Plus, he's Adam's closest friend, and he wants him here."

Despite being blindsided by this, it also doesn't escape my notice that there is no place setting for an eighth person. "He's not bringing a plus one?"

She gives a one shoulder shrug. "Seems that way."

"Does he know I'm going to be here?"

"To be honest, I'm not entirely certain how Adam spun it to him. I don't know if he assumes it's going to be just the three of us, like the other evening."

I look over in Adam's direction and see that he's in conversation with Pete. Nonetheless, my increasing curiosity makes me call out to him. "Hey, Adam, can you come and clarify something over here."

His eyes dart over to us, his dark brows rise inquiringly, his mouth twitching with amusement, as he walks over to us. His powerful well-muscled body moving towards us with ease. The man is seriously good looking. He places an arm around Jules's waist and kisses the top of her head. "Lauren, to what do I owe the pleasure of your summons."

"Two words. Mark Taylor."

He shares a smile with Jules, a look of complete and utter devotion. Then she nudges him in the side. "Ah, yes, he's been a little down lately, and quite frankly, I can't put up with his sulkiness any longer. It's fucking driving me mad. So can the two of you just kiss and make up already?"

"So inviting him here is your attempt at trying to get us back together? Does he know about this?"

"Not exactly. I invited him for dinner to cheer him up. He just assumed it would be the three of us."

"And you didn't see fit to correct him?"

"Nope." There's a knock at the door and a gleeful look of triumph accompanies his smile, denoting complete satisfaction with his subterfuge, as the grin spreads across his face. "Ah, speak of the devil." He wanders off to answer the door.

Mark makes his entrance as we're hovering at the table about to sit down. I notice the faint look of hopefulness, as his eyes scan the room when he realises he's not the only guest. When they fall on Pete, he doesn't even flinch. When his dark eyes fall on me, they become unfathomable.

He walks towards Pete, holding out his hand as he approaches him, his words said cool and clear. "I know your fist is acquainted with my jaw but let me officially introduce myself. Mark Taylor."

There's silence all around as we all wait with bated breath for Pete's reaction. He throws his head back and lets out a great burst of laughter, then extends his hand to meet Mark's. Unlike the last time they met, his voice and demeanour are more friendly. "Peter Roberts. And I have a sneaky suspicion it hurt me more than it hurt you."

Mark's face splits into a wide grin. When he finally turns to acknowledge me properly, his amusement is replaced with a smouldering look, but I detect the slight hint of hesitation.

His voice is smooth with a tinge of tenderness. "Lauren, it's really good to see you. You're looking as beautiful as ever."

I'm fixated, almost hypnotized, so that I don't say anything as his eyes hold mine. I notice the flicker of appreciation as I'm swept into the depths of his brilliant brown eyes. I'm so mesmerized that when Adam gives a loud clap to get our attention, I'm startled by the sound.

"Come on, let's sit down to eat. I haven't slaved over a hot stove and wasted my culinary skills for the food to go cold," he says.

I've tasted his food—he's an accomplished cook. The menu is a mix of his America-Italian roots. He's made us an appetizer of *insalata*, a lasagne for our main, and there's pecan pie for dessert, although I suspect that's something he's picked up from the local bakery.

Adam and Jules sit at opposite ends of the rectangle table. I sit next to Tom. Mark immediately takes the seat to my right sitting opposite Rachel who is seated next to Peter.

"This looks delicious," Tom says. "The only problem is you're setting a precedent, and I'm not sure my cooking skills are up to scratch."

"Don't worry. It's not your cooking skills that have endeared you to me," says Rachel.

"Thanks, Rach. Good to know I'm satisfying at least one of your appetites."

"Too much information, guys," I say.

"How long before you fly off to your next assignment,

Pete?" asks Jules.

"I'm off in a couple of weeks, to the Maldives actually, for a fashion shoot."

"Lucky son of a bitch," says Tom.

I'm about to put a forkful of food in my mouth but am halted by his surprise statement. I instantly look up as I place my knife and fork down and lean forward, staring inquisitively. A mixture of excitement for him and irritation that I'm only finding this out now. "Hang on, why am I just hearing about this? Does Mum know?"

"Keep your knickers on, Sis, I only found out this morning."

I narrow my eyes, shooting him a disgruntled look, letting him know I am not amused. His reaction is to turn his smile up a notch, knowing full well I can't stay angry with him for too long.

I'm conscious of Mark as he shifts in his seat and drapes his arm across the back of my chair. As I sit back, I'm not sure if it's accidental or not, but his fingers gently brush my bare arm, making my skin tingle and giving me a warm feeling, reminding me of everything about him that I've missed.

Mark skilfully changes the subject. "Jules, do you know what you're having? Are the pink flowers a hint?"

Adam chimes in. "A baby I should hope." He looks across the table at Jules, his eyes seeming to devour her beauty. She's glowing, even more beautiful in her pregnant state. She gazes back at him dreamily, the two of them momentarily lost in a world all of their own until the clattering of cutlery breaks their trance. "Although, if your recent mood swings are anything to go by, this kid is going to be trouble," he says.

"Only if it's a boy. If it's a girl, she'll be the epitome of prim and proper and the apple of her daddy's eye. And if you'd keep me stocked up with raspberry-flavoured twizzles, then I won't get moody. Just saying."

"So you don't know the sex?" asks Rachel.

"Sex. Did someone say sex."

I turn to my side, glaring at Mark in admonishment, unable to hold back the strong tone of disapproval in my voice. "Oh my God, trust you and your one-track mind. Anyone would think you were thirteen years old."

"Well, sex is what got them into this predicament." A chuckle of laughter accompanies his statement.

"It's not a predicament. It's a baby. A wonderful gift and an exciting time in their lives. You of all people should be able to relate to that. I can't believe you would even—"

There's a dose of impatience with a pinch of mockery thrown in for good measure. "For God's sake, it was a bloody joke. You've already been told not to get your knickers in a twist."

"I'm not doing this."

"Doing what?"

"Stooping to your level of immaturity."

He's grinning at me as if this is all one big fat joke. "I think you're too late on that score."

Before I can reply, Pete interrupts. "Now, now, children, let's not throw our toys out of the pram," he says.

I'm suddenly aware of the whole table watching us. Each and every one of them with a look of amusement, but Jules in particular is watching us with a look of enthrallment.

Mark leans in, gives my arm a reassuring squeeze as he whispers to me. His voice soft and genuinely apologetic. "I'm teasing you. I'm not trying to be malicious or mean. I'm sorry if I upset you."

I let out a deep sigh. "You have a funny way of showing it."

"I'm just a bundle of nerves. I didn't expect to see you here, and it's taken me by surprise." I find his admission of nervousness hard to believe.

"You, nervous? There's a turn-up for the books." But his regret is clearly genuine, so it's with the same conviction that I readily admit the truth. "I wasn't expecting you to be here either. It's rattled me a little. I'm sorry too for reacting the way I did. I know you're not trying to be deliberately cruel. Maybe just think before you speak next time."

He nods in acknowledgement. The warmth of his smile echoes in his voice as he seems to relax in relief. "I think Adam and Jules have surpassed themselves this time. I suspect there's an ulterior motive for this evening's dinner."

I look over at Jules and smile as the sound of laughter fills the room. "They mean well." We continue with our meal as the conversations around us flow.

"When are you flying back to the US?" asks Rachel.

I become momentarily speechless in surprise at this. "You're flying back to have the baby? Why am I the last to know everything? Did you know?" I look to Mark but don't wait for his answer.

Jules looks over at Adam, who is watching her adoringly. "Nothing is decided yet. It's still under debate," she says.

"I want my kid to have a shot at being president. And that can only happen if he's born in the US."

Jules rolls her eyes. "I'm sure he or she will have every opportunity afforded to them wherever they're born."

My heart swells for them. I know Jules will give Adam

what he wants. She's just having a little fun getting him riled up.

CHAPTER 27
Lauren

As the evening goes on, and we're finished with dinner, any atmosphere between me and Mark at the beginning has lightened up with the odd quip here and there. He's always been able to make me laugh. Being here with him, after weeks of being without him, reminds me of his fun side. It reminds me how much I miss him. How much I still want him. Leaving me to wonder if I'll ever get over him.

We move from the dining area to the living area, and I sink into the comfort of one of the two, three-seater sofas. In a flash, before anyone else can take the position next to me, Mark drops down beside me, sitting pretty close so his thigh is ever so lightly brushing against mine, causing me to angle a glance at him only to find his deliciously dark chocolate eyes studying me, making my heart flutter just a little.

"What?" I say quietly.

His lips curl upwards, as he flashes that boyish grin at me. "It's just really good to see you. I've missed you."

I let out a breath and take a moment before I answer. My eyes glued to his face, his lingering gaze tugging at my heart. I remember how those eyes would sensuously roam my body. The memory of his mouth on mine and how his hands would caress my body gives me shivers as I recall our intimate moments.

"Why are you telling me that?"

"I don't know. I suppose I just want you to know how I feel about you."

"I'm not doing this here."

"We can go out on the terrace for some privacy, if you like?"

I look over at the others. Rachel, Jules, and Tom are seated on the sofa opposite, with Adam sitting on the armrest, and Pete sitting on the floor, as the five of them chat away animatedly. I suspect they're deliberately pretending to not notice us talking.

Without saying a word, I slowly rise to my feet and take unhurried steps towards the French doors leading out to the terrace. Mark doesn't hesitate to follow me, his tall lithe figure moving eagerly.

I stand silently as Mark comes beside me, both of us taking in the envious night-time view, which I'm sure added a premium to the price of this apartment.

I glance at him, trying not to let my stare linger on him a moment longer than necessary in an attempt to hide my emotions. He doesn't need to know that every time I look at him, every time his eyes capture mine, my heart turns over.

"Well, what would you like to discuss? What is it you're expecting to gain from this little chat? That all will be forgiven, just like that?"

"I suppose I am hoping for that, yes."

He moves close to me. His eyes flicker as he looks at me intently. He's so handsome my heart lurches madly as I try my best not to get swept away in the depths of his appraising eyes.

"I just want you to myself for a while. I want to know if we can try and get past things. If you can forgive me and maybe give me another chance? I'll beg if I have to. I'm not beyond begging."

I contemplate what he's saying. Is what he's done so terrible? Is it unforgivable? After all, he's a father. He's just protecting his daughter and putting her needs and interests above his own.

People deserve a second chance, a do-over, don't they? Life doesn't always give you that second shot, but perhaps this is ours. Maybe Adam and Jules's sneaky attempt at playing cupid is a blessing in disguise because I know there's something between us worth another shot. But equally, he has to prove himself. But if Rose can forgive Dan, maybe I can give Mark a second chance.

"I don't think we should rush into anything. A lot has happened. I need you to prove that you're willing to put the time and effort into a relationship. Rose comes first. I get it. But you have to make time for me, not just for sex. There needs to be some major grovelling on your part before I can even contemplate thinking about giving you another chance."

"I'm willing to do whatever it takes to have you back in my life."

"Yes, but as what? I'm not prepared for us to go back to how it was. I don't want to be on speed dial when you need a good fuck. I want more."

"And you deserve more. I'll do my best to change."

"I don't want you to change per se. I just need you to show me that I matter, that you care. That this—us, is something you want."

"I'll do anything and everything for you."

"Wow! You said that without even throwing in a sexual connotation. You're making progress already."

"So you'll consider it?"

I take my eyes off him and look out over London. And give him my answer, my words echoing my own longing. "I'll think about it."

He smacks my butt. "Come on let's go back inside and join the fun and games."

When we get back inside there's some sort of "what if" game going on. "Would you rather be invisible for a day or have the power to read someone's mind?" Rachel asks the group.

"Invisible. I already know how you think," says Tom.

She gives him a loving smile before her next question. "Mark, if you won the lottery what's the first thing you would buy?"

He smiles as he thinks for a split second before answering. "Money can't buy what I want."

CHAPTER 28
Mark

I've spent the last week inside my head, examining my own thoughts and feelings, reflecting on my mistakes. Trying to only think of the positives and not dwell on regrets. Because I certainly would regret not reaching out. I would forever regret not using my entire arsenal to try and win her back.

Despite how well I thought things went at the dinner party, I haven't been able to pin Lauren down to go on a date. She's only returned one of my numerous calls. Maybe it's a test. Bring it on. I do my best work under pressure.

I've sent enough bouquets of flowers to her workplace and her apartment to fill a football stadium; the fact that I practically bought out the florist's entire stock should entitle me to shares in the place.

I know she's deliberately playing hard to get, but who can blame her. But how long can she keep this up? The old me would let it drag out, but the new me, the *in love* me, doesn't want to waste any more precious time.

I realise that the difference in me is because I'm in love. I'm only sorry that it's taken me so long to get my arse into gear.

As soon as I admitted to myself that I want Lauren to be a part of my life permanently, it was like a weight lifted from my shoulders. I realised that the everyday mundane stuff doesn't seem to bother you so much when you know that there's someone who loves you—flaws and all. It's a freeing feeling, like a bird, ready to take flight to wherever love will take me. Although there is only one place I want to be, and that's with Lauren, holding her tight in the comfort of my arms, never letting go. Jesus Christ, I've become like a lovesick teenager, and I don't give a damn, because it feels fucking great.

So yesterday I took back control, and I called and asked her to lunch, but she said no. I had a moment of deflation and panic until she suggested coffee instead at a quaint independent coffee shop local to where she lives.

I arrive an eager ten minutes early, pleased to be able to choose a table in the corner. As soon as I see her walk in, I push myself to a standing position. I'm conscious of the wide grin on my face as she approaches, I'm just so fucking grateful she's shown up. That must mean something. When I see her smile break though the uncertainty, that gives me hope.

She looks so incredible that I'm using all of my self-control not to pounce on her. Instead, I lean in to kiss her and am overjoyed that she doesn't seem to object when my lips place a gentle kiss on her cheek. "It's good to see you," I say.

She replies with that sultry voice of hers, "You, too." She sits in the chair as I go to the counter to order our coffees.

I return and place her cup down in front of her. "I got you a flat white."

She looks up at me. "You remember. Thanks."

I feel pleased with myself for the extra points gained. "Thanks for meeting me."

She adds a sachet of brown sugar to her coffee and stirs. "I have to admit I'm curious. I thought I made my feelings clear at the dinner party about what I want—what I'm not willing to accept. It's going to take more than a few bunches of flowers."

"Yeah, I get that. We've had some real shit go on, and I know it's all my fault. I hate the fact that I've hurt you. If I could undo everything I would. I love you, and if you let me, I promise I'll spend the rest of my life making it up to you."

I watch as her reaction to those three little words sink in. She dismissed them last time I said them, perhaps not quite believing them, and who could blame her.

Her eyes glaze. I know she's trying to fight her own emotions. I'm going to need all of my masterful persuasion to win her back. She takes a breath to speak, but I place my hand over hers to stop her.

 "Let me finish. What I'm trying to say is that it's always been you, Lauren. Right from the very start, from our very first incredible night together. It's always been you and only you. I'm not happy to live my life without you, not now, not after meeting you. I want you in my world—in my life. You don't belong in my past. You belong in my here and now, in my future."

She laces her fingers with mine as a flicker of a smile plays on the corners of her mouth, and she watches me through lowered lashes.

"I've finally realised that there's enough love to go around. They're two separate relationships, but I'd like to amalgamate them."

Her eyes dart up as she lets go of my hands. "That's very generous of you."

"Fuck, sorry, wrong choice of words. What I'm trying to say is that I don't want you to give up on us. I want us to be a family. Do you think we could be a family, the three us?"

There's a slither of a smirk as she studies my face, looking into my eyes, searching for the sincerity that I hope I'm projecting. Praying she can feel the love gushing from every pore in my body.

Her hands are wrapped around her cup, and she stares into her coffee as she speaks. "I didn't expect to fall in love with Rose. I kept my expectations realistic. At the very least, I thought she would tolerate me if she had to. But we seem to have bonded."

"Rose wants to send you an invite to her sixteenth birthday party. I thought perhaps you could come as my date."

She looks up at me, a slow steady smile of happiness appearing. God, I've missed that smile. "I'd love to come. But not as your date."

I'm silenced by her response. Is she shooting me down? Is that it? We're done? The tensing of my jaw conceals my sadness. But she seems to notice my disappointment of having my hopes dashed.

"I'll come with Adam and Jules. I don't think we should run before we can walk, do you?"

My mood is suddenly buoyant at being given a lifeline. I can't help but let my happiness and relief shine through as I grin from ear to ear. "No, you're right. As always. However you want to do this. We can go as slow as you like."

"Good. So how is Rose? Is she excited about her party?"

"Yeah, she's pretty hyper about it all. She's seeing that

Dan boy. Not something I'm entirely happy about, but I'm trying to be a little more easy going. If I've learnt anything, it's that Rose has a good head on her shoulders. Something you were able to see before me."

"Don't beat yourself up about it. Some things are easier to see when you're looking in from the outside. Also she's headstrong, just like her dad. That's a useful trait sometimes. The main thing is you got there in the end."

"I'm hoping we can get there in the end."

"We will. Let's take it slow. As if we've just met. Maybe after Rose's party you can ask me out on a proper date."

"God, I fucking love you."

With softness in her hazel eyes, she looks at me dreamily as she places a hand on my thigh. "I love you too. All I ever wanted was for you to fight for me. Prove yourself. Show me you want me, want there to be an us badly enough to not give up."

Her words are reassuring, and I feel a powerful relief. "I'll never give up on us. Christ, I want kiss you. You have no idea what you're doing to me right now. Fuck, I'm so hard I feel like I'm going to burst."

She removes her hand from my thigh. There's a trace of laughter in her voice, and her lashes flutter, almost hypnotizing me. "Hmm, I'm not sure they'd appreciate our X-rated displays of affection here. Enough about us. Why don't we change the subject, alleviate the horniness you have going on."

I shift in my seat for relief, and while my mind is telling me to resist, my body is telling me otherwise, so I move my chair just a little so that the temptation is just out of reach. "Sure. How have you been generally? I've been keeping an eye on your latest campaign. It seems to be going well."

Her eyes light up with enthusiasm. "Oh my God. I can't believe how well it's going."

It's the oddest thing. Once we've gotten the awkward stuff out of the way, we seem to fall into an easy flow of conversation, and it's with some reluctance that we finally end the date.

***

It's been two days since I laid my cards on the table, and Rose's party isn't for another two weeks. But I don't think I can wait that long to see Lauren again. I refuse to wait any longer to hold her. I just want to kiss her, make love to her. But, at the same time, I'm nervous. Perhaps, despite everything she said, she's unable to forgive me. I can't forgive myself for the way I've behaved. I would certainly make my displeasure known if Rose was being treated the way I'd treated Lauren. But the first step to forgiveness is admitting and accepting your mistakes. Or maybe it's simply that she doesn't feel the same anymore. But I quickly discard that notion when I recall the way she placed her hand on my thigh and the way her eyes looked deep into mine, full of promise, full of love.

Which is why I've finally decided to take decisive action. I'm going to go get the woman once and for all. That's the reason why I'm now standing on her doorstep, with Rose tagging along for moral support. So much for being confident and assertive. You could say I'm a bundle of nerves.

As I walk up to the front door my heart is pounding and my stomach is churning. I'm feeling like a lovesick teen, knocking on his date's front door, anticipating being confronted by an overprotective father, something I know I'm going to have to deal with in the not too distant future.

"Go on, ring the doorbell, Dad," Rose calls from behind the bush in next-door's front garden.

I've learnt my lesson over the last few months, so I do as I'm told and ring the doorbell. My excuse for coming here is to hand deliver her invite. Yeah, I know, as I said, desperate. And I can't even take credit; it was Rose's idea.

"Hello." Her soft voice comes over the intercom.

"Hey. It's me," I say.

"Mark? Give me a second. I'll come down."

Is that a bad sign? Why didn't she just buzz me in? Does she have someone up there? Another man? As I wait on the doorstep, staring at the door, my nerves are getting the better of me. I take in every crack, every bit of flaky paint. I can see her shadow through the stained glass of the door. When she opens the door, she smiles at me. Unsure of what's coming, she looks down at the ground, her hand brushing a lock of hair behind her ear.

"Hi, I erm… I came to give you this." I pull out the slightly crumpled envelope from my back pocket and hand it to her."

She looks up at me with questioning eyes. "What is it?"

"Your invitation to Rose's party. Remember, you said you'd come."

A smile creeps across her face as she hears Rose call out, "Kiss her, kiss her." And then she suddenly flings herself at me, putting her arms around my neck and kissing me, right there on the doorstep, with no complaints from me.

As I wrap my arms around her and hold her tight, I inhale her intoxicating scent. It reminds me of carefree childhood summers. It brings to mind visions of daisies. She leans back to look at me, her long lashes flutter as she blinks, holding me spellbound. As I look deeper into her eyes, they reveal to me everything I need to know, and when she kisses me again, it's like no other sensation I've ever had. Her tender kiss has my heart pounding, it sends currents of desire coursing through me, proving to me I'm right where I belong, with who I belong.

As her sweet lips feed mine like a man starved, Rose is in the background clapping with joy, which makes us reluctantly pull apart.

"Did you put your dad up to this?"

Rose gives a shrug of indifference, giving the appearance of taking it all in her stride as if it's an everyday occurrence.

But it's not. Winning back Lauren's affections, her forgiveness, is not something I intend to take for granted. I'm not saying I'm going to have a complete personality transplant, but I will let her know every day how much I love her and how much she means to me, and Rose for that matter. She's been as determined as me to win Lauren back. For us to be a family.

EPILOGUE
Mark

"For crying out loud, are you ready yet? We're going to be late. The godparents can't be late," she calls out from the living room.

Typical Lauren. Straight in for the jugular. God, I love her.

Yep, Adam and Jules had a baby boy. And yes, he'll have a shot at being president one day if that's the path he chooses.

I place the small ring box in the breast pocket of my suit jacket and walk casually from the bedroom to join her as she stands impatiently waiting for me.

"About time. And they say women take forever to get ready."

"Jesus Christ, woman, will you stop nagging. I don't want a nagger; you could at least have the decency to wait until the fucking ring is on your finger."

Her demeanour changes. She tilts her head as her brows rise a fraction, and she shoots me a quizzical look. Her mouth opens and closes in surprise as she weighs up what I've just said. Granted, it's not how I planned to propose.

"Is that a proposal, Mark Taylor?"

I answer instantly with emphasis. "Yes, it bloody well is. And don't you dare complain about my delivery." I take out the small box and open it to reveal a pear shaped diamond ring.

Her beautiful smile widens, and it reaches her eyes as

she looks at the ring then back at me. "I'm not complaining."

"Good."

"Good."

My gaze is steady, capturing her eyes with mine. "So what's your answer?"

Her voice softens. "You do look incredibly handsome."

She inches nearer to me and straightens my tie. Then her hands palm my face as her mouth covers mine. The feel of her warm lips on mine as she gently presses a kiss on my lips feels as though it's our first kiss. It's only supposed to be a quick peck, but my arms slide around her waist, pulling her tightly to me. She wraps her arms around my neck, and I revel in the velvety warmth of her kiss as her lips caress mine. I follow her lead in this merry dance as her lips part and her tongue coaxes my lips open. It's a deep kiss. Our tongues stimulating each other to a new high as they swirl in circles. All the while she's caressing the back of my neck while I can't help myself as I grab her butt, pulling her even closer so that she can feel my hardness against her thigh, letting her know exactly what she does to me.

My emotions are whirling, creating a burning desire, an aching need to take her right here, right now. To give her everything and anything she wants.

When we break the kiss, I look at her expectantly.

Her eyes stare back at me, her brow raised questioningly. "What?"

My arms are still firmly around her waist, holding her tight to me. "I take it that's a yes?"

She gently brushes her fingers through my hair as she rewards me with her words. "Of course. It's all in the kiss."

As I slip the ring on her finger, I smile to myself, forever thankful for her stubbornness, forever grateful that she never gave up on me, on us, and our little family. "I want you to kiss me like that for a lifetime."

"I'll see what I can do."

***

Thank you for reading. I hope you enjoyed Mark and Lauren's story.

You can read Adam and Jules's story in **Love Unexpected**.

Get it here: https://books2read.com/loveunexpected

***

Reviews are super important for an indie author. If you enjoyed this book I would be forever grateful if you could take a few minutes to leave a review (it can be as short as you like). Thank you. Stay happy. Keep reading.

GOODREADS

http://bit.ly/marina-goodreads

BOOKBUB

http://bit.ly/marina-bookbub

AMAZON

US: https://www.amazon.com/MARINA-HANNA/e/B07P5F1PX1

UK: https://www.amazon.co.uk/MARINA-HANNA/e/B07P5F1PX1

***

Connect/Follow Marina
https://marinahannaauthor.com
https://www.instagram.com/marinac2003
email: authormarinahanna@yahoo.com

MARINA HANNA

http://bit.ly/marina-goodreads
http://bit.ly/marina-bookbub
Sign up for my newsletter: http://eepurl.com/ggcgsX

***

Editing: Hot Tree Editing
Cover: www.timelesspremades.com

Printed in Great Britain
by Amazon